MIRACULOUS

ALSO BY CAROLINE STARR ROSE

Jasper and the Riddle of Riley's Mine
Blue Birds
May B.

MIRACULOUS

Caroline Starr Rose

putnam

G. P. PUTNAM'S SONS

G. P. PUTNAM'S SONS

An imprint of Penguin Random House LLC, New York

First published in the United States of America by G. P. Putnam's Sons,
an imprint of Penguin Random House LLC, 2022

Visit us online at penguinrandomhouse.com

Library of Congress Cataloging-in-Publication Data
Names: Rose, Caroline Starr, author.
Title: Miraculous / Caroline Starr Rose.
Description: New York: G. P. Putnam's Sons, [2022] | Summary: A traveling
medicine show promises to cure all that ails, but thirteen-year-old Jack and his friend
Cora learn it takes more than faith in the miraculous to fix things that are broken.
Identifiers: LCCN 2022011427 (print) | LCCN 2022011428 (ebook) |
ISBN 9781984813152 (hardcover) | ISBN 9781984813169 (ebook)
Subjects: CYAC: Medicine shows—Fiction. | Friendship—Fiction. | Secrets—Fiction. |
Mystery and detective stories. | Detective and mystery stories.
Classification: LCC PZ7.R71464 Mi 2022 (print) | LCC PZ7.R71464 (ebook) |
DDC [Fic]—dc23
LC record available at https://lccn.loc.gov/2022011427
LC ebook record available at https://lccn.loc.gov/2022011428

Book manufactured in Canada

ISBN 9781984813152
1 3 5 7 9 10 8 6 4 2
FRI

Design by Suki Boynton • Text set in Baskerville

For Valerie Geary—wise writer, dear friend

MIRACULOUS

OAKDALE

THE SILENT DAWN trailed Jack down Main Street, crept with him as he slipped his paste brush across each hand-bill and smoothed the dampened paper flat. The stillness drew near as he hung signs on walls and hitching posts. It shadowed him from the feedstore's steps to the dim light of the bakery.

For more than a year he'd been with the doctor. He'd spent his thirteenth birthday far from home. In that time, Jack had visited plenty of places, too many for him to re-member. Still he cherished the first morning in a new town, where the quiet was held as close as a secret.

He'd left the wagon in the early gray light not far from the entrance of town. A stack of paper tucked under his arm. The glue bucket bumping against his knee. He was a messenger, Isaac said, whose handbills announced the doctor's arrival.

Isaac would be in the graveyard now. This was how it always began. Once the two of them finished their work, they'd meet up with the doctor again.

Jack pasted two signs on the general store, one at eye level for the adults, one low enough for the children to see. He'd post them on each storefront and window, enough that news of the show couldn't be missed. That was something Isaac had taught him. The faster word spread, the bigger the crowd. If sales of the tonic started strong, they would stay in a town a couple of weeks.

Jack hung more signs near the darkened alley. He posted them by the stables, too. Like other places they'd stopped, Oakdale had raised wooden sidewalks and a road that ran through the center of town. But something felt different about this place. Shops huddled together like birds on a fence. The church bell tilted as though it had stopped in midswing. The towering tree in the center of town lifted its limbs in expectation while its red leaves reached for the sky.

A flash of fur caught his eye. An old stray. He'd seen it by the bank, and now the dog was following him. Jack set down his pail and held out his hand. Slowly, the dog crept closer. It brushed its gray muzzle across Jack's palm and thumped its burr-tangled tail.

He stroked the stray's back. "You've seen a lot of years, haven't you, boy?"

The dog pricked its ears with listening.

Jack took in the dog, the tilt of its head, the sturdy set of its chin. He tried to see it as Isaac had taught him, to observe everything he could. The dog might have been old, but it was still watchful. Though age had stiffened its joints, its determination stayed strong.

Sun streaked across Main Street's windows. Jack pressed the last handbill to a pane of glass. Behind him, papers brightened the storefronts like snowflakes heralding a storm. He relished the thought of snow and the cold. The morning was already hot; the day would only grow hotter. Jack couldn't remember an October like this one, where the summer heat had never ended and it hadn't rained since spring.

He gazed into the stray's rheumy eyes. The dog was a good one, the faithful kind—as if a dog could be anything else. What had it seen in its years in town? What would it say if it could speak? Jack scratched the old dog under its chin. "Nothing's the same once the doctor arrives. Just you wait and see."

A SUDDEN DEPARTURE

MEET AT THE grove, the doctor had said. It didn't take Jack long to find the willows near the riverbank. From the road, he spied the wagon tucked beneath a curtain of branches and the chestnut mare grazing nearby. A clearing opened under the trees, the dry grass dappled in shadow.

Jack rounded the path to the grove, empty bucket in hand. Closer he came. Something rippled the branches. A shout rang out that sounded like Isaac. He was already back?

Jack made out the form of a tall, gaunt man. "Dr. Kingsbury?" he called. "Are you there?"

A hand brushed the branches aside, revealing the doctor in his long black coat. He wore the dress coat for every occasion, no matter the season or weather. Behind him was Isaac, his head bowed.

"You're back." The doctor's dark eyes met his own. "I take it you've finished the notices."

"Yes," Jack said.

"Did you hear that, Isaac? He's already done."

Deep in his pockets, Isaac's hands curled to fists. "Don't do this. Not in front of Jack."

Dr. Kingsbury tucked his black hair behind one ear. "Why should that make a difference? He did what I told him, while you—"

"He doesn't need to—"

"Hear what you said? What you accused me of? Believe me, I won't repeat that."

Isaac's cheek burned red. The doctor had hit him.

"Please go." Isaac stared at Jack, his blue eyes pleading. "Down to the river. I'll come find you later, all right?"

Jack dropped the bucket, the paste brush clattering inside. He ran down the path to the riverbank.

This wasn't the first time they'd argued, the doctor and Isaac. It wasn't the first time the doctor had hit him. Isaac often spoke his mind. In the last weeks, he'd grown even bolder. The doctor blamed Isaac turning sixteen and the two days he'd spent in Greenville visiting his cousin.

Jack pulled himself up on a slab of stone and watched the water flow by. For all the parts where the river raced, there were as many spots where it pooled and slowed. Sometimes Dr. Kingsbury could be harsh, but he'd never tried to hurt Jack. In his year on the road, Jack had learned to be thorough and prompt with his chores. More than once, Isaac had taken the blame when Jack made a mistake.

Jack waited and waited for Isaac to come, was waiting still when the sun reached its peak. It was only then he let himself think it: Isaac wasn't coming for him. He made his way back to the grove, unsure of what he'd find.

All was silent in the clearing, a world away from the noise of the river. The wagon, like a small house on wheels, was sheltered under the willow trees. The mare grazed near its lacquered door.

Jack climbed to the wagon's porch, the steps creaking under his feet. He knocked on the door and opened it, though he wasn't supposed to go in alone.

Surely the doctor would be hard at work, counting the bottles inside. Every stop in a town always started the same. Dr. Kingsbury had checked them once in Greenville, but a single count was never enough. The first, done by the glassmaker, was suspect. Merchants were bent on making a profit and sometimes sold fewer bottles than promised. The second count, taken soon after, uncovered such deceit. But the third count showed his true inventory. That was the number the doctor recorded, after travel or distance or ruts in the road chipped bottles or sent others crashing down, shattering them on the wagon's floor.

One could never be too careful, the doctor always said.

"Hello? Dr. Kingsbury?" Slowly Jack's eyes adjusted to the wagon's dim interior. A spicy tang filled the air, a scent Isaac once said was ginger mixed with snakeroot.

The doctor set down his herb-filled mortar. Candles cast shadows on his angled face. "So you didn't run off with him."

"Run off?" Jack wasn't sure he'd heard correctly.

"You didn't run off with Isaac."

It made no sense, what the doctor was saying. "What? Isaac? He wouldn't . . ."

The doctor unlocked a drawer in his desk, a drawer Jack and Isaac were never to touch. Inside was the money pouch, empty. "He's run off. For good. I gave him a minute to gather himself and what did he do? He left with my money."

That didn't sound like Isaac at all. He'd worked for the doctor long before Jack. He hadn't said much at breakfast, but that was no different from other mornings when they woke well before dawn. Isaac had pulled on his shoes and cinched his bag tight with the string he kept tied to the shoulder strap. "Until after," he'd said, giving Jack a salute.

"Until after," Jack had answered.

They started mornings in a new town this way—a

7

send-off that meant they'd meet up again soon. There'd been nothing unusual about last night, either, when they'd worked on their carvings on the wagon's porch. Isaac's wooden rabbit was so full of life, it looked ready to leap from his hand.

Stars had pierced the heavens. The lanterns had swung on the eaves above, keeping time with the horse as they'd traveled. The world had been as small as the wagon, as grand as the sparkling sky. They'd talked of what might happen in town. Would people be wary when they first glimpsed the doctor with his wild hair and long, dark coat? Or would they take to him right from the start? Some were cautious when the doctor arrived, but Jack had never seen Dr. Kingsbury fail to win a town over.

Nothing about last night seemed out of place. Maybe Isaac needed some time alone. Or maybe he'd had enough. Had he really left? Was he finished?

The doctor shook his head as though trying to clear it. "What's done is done. What have you found?"

It was one of Jack's responsibilities, learning about the new place they'd stopped. He cast his thoughts back to what he'd seen. "Oakdale's getting on better than Ashland, but it's not as well-off as Greenville." Ashland, a town where they'd stopped in July, was six weathered storefronts on a long dusty road. But Greenville, the last town where they'd stayed, was the county seat. It had a train station, the sheriff's office, a three-story courthouse, and a fancy hotel with brass knockers on the doors.

"Oakdale's right in the middle, then, a place where meals aren't hard to come by. Remember this, Jack. A man whose focus is getting his supper pays no mind to much else. Well-fed towns take the most interest in tonic."

Jack was no longer surprised by the doctor's observations. Once, when they'd passed an abandoned barn, the doctor had later asked him about it. Jack had only remembered its sagging roof, but the doctor had talked of its promise. The barn could serve as a shelter from rain or a haven on a winter night. Its planks could be fashioned into a bench or laid over puddles on a mud-bogged road. Opportunity was everywhere, Dr. Kingsbury said. It could be found in the simplest things.

The doctor shook herbs into the mortar and crushed them under the pestle's blunt end. "I want you near the square an hour before the show begins."

Jack's stomach lurched. "That's Isaac's job."

"And now it's yours." The doctor added a sprinkle of powder and stirred the mixture again.

Jack's job was to hang signs and paste labels. Rinse bottles and fill them with tonic. He'd never talked to the crowds before.

"Make sure the people on Main Street see you. Tell the children leaving school to come to the square. And with every person you meet, be certain to speak of the tonic."

"Dr. Kingsbury's Miraculous Tonic," Jack recited automatically. "Relieves every malady known to man or beast."

The doctor studied him carefully. "You've been listening, then."

Jack wasn't sure how the medicine worked, but he knew it remedied all kinds of ailments. It had cured Lucy's fever when she lay abed, when the family had worried she might never get well.

Sweet Lucy, his baby sister. He missed her, being so far away. But Jack owed so much to Dr. Kingsbury, who'd given him tonic when he'd had no money. Then the doctor had offered him a job. Every month, Jack sent his pay home to his family. A year and a half, the doctor had said, maybe a little more. By then they'd circle back to Covington, and Jack would be home, free to leave his job or stay on if he wanted.

Dr. Kingsbury pushed aside the tails of his coat and settled on a stool. "You must raise your voice to draw a crowd. Once you're sure you've been heard, shout even louder. When you spy a youth with blemishes or a man who bears an unsightly scar, tell them the tonic not only aids pain but soothes conditions of the flesh." The doctor stared at him, unblinking. "Remember, Jack, the crowd rests on your shoulders now."

The ill, the needy, the weary of heart. Isaac had found

the afflicted and gathered them in. Was he really gone? Had he taken the money? Why wasn't the doctor looking for him?

It wasn't like Isaac to leave Jack with his work, to run off without saying goodbye.

DREAMS AND DARES

CORA'S BOOTS SMACKED the ground as she raced through the alley. Her breath came steady and strong. Each morning she got a little faster, went farther than the day before. If Mother knew, she wouldn't approve. Nettie, her cousin, wouldn't understand. A young lady of Oakdale didn't act like a child or—worse—like an unruly boy. Girls didn't run, simple as that. But for Cora it was her chance at adventure. For the length of the alley, those rules didn't matter. Running took her away to a world of her choosing.

She slowed as the alley spilled onto Main Street. It was almost eight. The shops were still closed. Cora loved this time of morning best, when shadows altered the places she knew. Instead of the sawmill, she imagined a library with stately columns supporting its roof. If she squinted a little, the church's spire turned into a building that touched the clouds.

It wasn't that Cora didn't like Oakdale. She just wanted more. There were dozens of other towns in Ohio. A thousand places she hoped to visit.

The sun hadn't been up very long, but already its heat burned the back of her neck. It felt like an August afternoon, not an October morning. If only it would rain again. They hadn't had any since spring. For weeks, the sky had been nothing but empty, but today, clouds ran in fine, bold strokes that flared to wispy tails. Hadn't Nana taught her to read the clouds? Change was certainly near.

It was then she noticed the handbills that covered the storefronts and hitching posts. As she neared Miss Moore's shop, she realized each handbill had the same message stamped in the middle. Cora picked up one that had fallen:

SICK HEADACHE? SOUR STOMACH? WEAK NERVES? RHEUMATISM? GENERAL MALAISE?

SUFFER NO MORE!
DR. KINGSBURY HAS THE ANSWERS.
MEET IN THE SQUARE AT THREE O'CLOCK.

They hadn't been there yesterday. It was a little unsettling to imagine a person, this Dr. Kingsbury, whoever he was, sneaking around as she slept. Unsettling, but also mysterious.

A stranger, come from another place.

If Oakdale had rules about running, for outsiders there were a hundred rules more. Strangers could visit, but they weren't meant to stay. It was better to hold them at a distance. They certainly couldn't announce on a notice they'd host their own gathering in Founder's Square. Cora tried to remember if she'd ever heard of a doctor visiting town before. The closest one she knew lived in Cleveland. Mostly people relied on family remedies or the help of neighbors when sickness came.

She folded the handbill and lifted her face to the swirling clouds. Maybe today would mark the end of the drought. Cora closed her eyes, dreaming. A delightful shiver passed through her.

The clouds that hinted at rain, perhaps they bespoke something more.

She'd give anything for a taste of the world. Now a bit of the world was coming to Oakdale.

Maybe if she showed Nettie the notice, she'd want to see the doctor, too. Cora put it in her pocket and let her feet fly. Out in the open, down the middle of Main Street. She'd keep running until she reached school. What did it matter if Reverend Wells spotted her or Father saw her as he opened his store? Let the whole town take note. Let them report back to Mother if they wished.

None of that mattered. Today marked a new beginning. A day for dreams and dares.

A DISMISSAL AVERTED

JACK HEARD THE crush of footsteps on the gravel road. All morning the grove had been quiet except for the murmuring river and the clink of bottles as he'd washed them in the tub.

Isaac was back! Of course he was. Dr. Kingsbury was somehow mistaken. Jack knew Isaac wouldn't leave him like that. He set down a newly rinsed bottle and started for the road. The missing coins he couldn't explain, but he knew Isaac wasn't a thief. Not once had he seen Isaac take any money, though there had been plenty of chances.

The grass rustled as the footsteps drew closer. It wasn't Isaac that Jack saw, but a broad-shouldered man, solid and stout, with a thick mustache set over a frown. In his hand he gripped a fistful of paper. "Did you have something to do with this?" The man shook the paper like it was aflame. "Are you the one who left these all over?"

"I, well, I . . ." Jack stepped away, but the man kept with him.

"Out with it, boy. Did you leave these or not?"

"I was just doing what the doctor asked."

The tips of the man's ears reddened. "You were asked to cover every wall and window in Oakdale with this rubbish? I wouldn't let the Ladies' Auxiliary announce their next tea without prior notice. Here you are, a nobody boy, cluttering my town with trash and gibberish about some Dr. Kingsbury, whom I don't know, who has no authority to—"

The wagon door opened. Dr. Kingsbury descended in smooth, soundless steps. His dark suit was immaculate. His eyes, darker still, were ever watchful. A twist in the bridge of his nose made Jack think it once had been broken. The doctor's black hair skimmed his shoulders. He wore a fresh poppy in his buttonhole. It had been weeks since they'd passed wildflowers dotting the roadside in yellows and reds, yet the poppy remained, bright and changeless.

"Welcome, sir." The doctor clasped the man's hand, crumpling the papers between them. "My notices, I see. Then you've heard of my show. Have you come to learn more?"

The man shook himself free of the doctor. "Explain this nonsense at once."

Now that Dr. Kingsbury had come, Jack wondered if he should excuse himself. This wasn't his concern. He should go.

Only he couldn't.

It didn't matter if the doctor was before one man or an entire crowd. He commanded the attention of all who were near, like an actor onstage. Jack had never been to a play, but Isaac had told him about one he'd seen. The play had been filled with surprises, with actors dressed in elaborate costumes who could make you gasp or laugh. An actor told a story, Isaac said, not only with words but with the wink of an eye, the turn of a hand.

Wasn't that just like the doctor?

His long limbs would have been awkward on anyone else, yet Dr. Kingsbury moved with precision and grace. If ever his audience thundered in doubt, the doctor's response was calm. No illness was too great, no weakness too strong that his remedy couldn't bring healing.

Dr. Kingsbury preached this above all.

"My name's Elijah Kingsbury. The people of Oakdale have need of me."

"And what would you know of Oakdale's needs?"

The doctor drew close to the man. "It's clear you care

for your town. Why else would you have sought me out? Are you a councilman? A member of the board?"

The man crossed his arms over his chest. "A councilman? Please. I'm Mayor Nathanael James."

"Forgive me, Mayor James," the doctor said, "I mean no disrespect. But surely you wouldn't deny the good people of Oakdale the chance to be healed?"

The mayor's ears turned a deeper red. "You know nothing about the concerns of this town."

"Every town is touched by calamity." The doctor placed a hand to his chest, his fingers in reach of the poppy's fine petals. "Heartache. Earache. Rheumatism. Wind colic disrupting the bowels. Sore throats, weak knees, or hens that've stopped laying. All of us suffer at one time or another. My tonic relieves every malady."

Show them their need. Provide them a cure. Some of the doctor's teachings Jack didn't quite grasp, but this one he understood. A person must recognize what they lacked to accept the good news of the tonic.

"It helped my sister. The tonic. It saved her." Jack hadn't known he'd speak until the words were halfway out. He remembered the backs of Lucy's hands, still dimpled like a baby's, the fine hair that curled over her ears. She had been two when he'd left home. Summertime fevers were known to pass quickly, but Lucy's had lingered for weeks.

The doctor's eyes softened as he took in Jack. "Mayor James, let me introduce my assistant."

"The boy and I have already met." The mayor's speech was clipped, but something had shifted. His face was less pinched. His frown had faded.

"Go on, Jack," the doctor said. "Tell us your story."

It was hard to think of those days without sadness, but in the remembering, Lucy felt near. "She took so sick she slept most of the time. She barely sipped the broth Ma made."

A breath of wind stirred the willow branches, a trace of coolness in the stifling heat.

"We heard a doctor had come to town. I went to his show and brought home some tonic. Dr. Kingsbury, when he heard about Lucy, gave me a bottle for free. Ma gave her a spoonful straightaway, and by supper Lu asked for some bread. Come morning, her fever had broken. The rattle in her chest was gone. It was miraculous, my papa said. The doctor's good medicine cured her."

Jack listened to the river as it slipped over stones, the same one they'd followed in their year on the road. The river ran through the valley near home. It was where he'd chased tadpoles and caught fish for supper, where he'd watched the sunset reflected like a field of stars.

"Bless the child," Mayor James said. "How does your sister fare now?"

"You've heard from your family, have you not?" Dr. Kingsbury asked.

Jack nodded. "I got a letter in Greenville. Ma said Lucy is healthy, as spirited as she was before."

He pictured Lucy sprawled on the rug, busy playing with a basket of buttons. He thought of her high baby voice, the funny words he understood even when his parents didn't. But Lu wouldn't be so little now. She was born the summer of 1884. That made her already three.

Mayor James blinked his dampened eyes. "Well, then. Kingsbury." He cleared his throat. "We have rules about outsiders here. How you entered town was not regulation. But I have children of my own. This boy's tale gives me something to think about. If what he's saying is true, Oakdale could use a bit of that. I'll make an exception this time."

"Thank you," Dr. Kingsbury said.

"You may hold your show in Founder's Square. Only be wise. I won't be this lenient again." The mayor nodded curtly. "Good day to you both."

Mayor James took the path back through the willows. "I thought he'd force us to leave," Jack said.

"He wasn't far from it."

"But you were able to settle him down."

"I reasoned with him, but you won him over."

"Me?" Jack said. "What do you mean?"

"You talked to him, appealed to his emotions, the way I taught Issac to do."

"But I'm nothing like Isaac."

Dr. Kingsbury scowled. "That's not a bad thing. The boy had grown self-important of late, convinced he knew best when he didn't. But you have something Isaac never had. A story of someone changed by my tonic."

Self-important. Was that what it was? Why Isaac had left without telling him? Jack had thought they'd been friends. He brushed his hand over his pocket, checking that his carving was there. If Isaac had run, as the doctor said, he wasn't the friend Jack had thought him to be.

Shadows marked the hollows of Dr. Kingsbury's cheeks. "We'll make Lucy's story a part of the show. Beginning this afternoon."

IN NEED OF WORK

THE BOY WALKED the road, his boots dirty and worn, toward the oak in the center of town. No one was willing to take him on, not the storekeeper, the blacksmith, or even the barber. He could clean up the floor—the boy knew how to sweep—but the barber said help wasn't needed.

Three days he'd been traveling; he was three days from home, and the ache of it stung like his blistered feet. Partly because he couldn't find work. Partly because he was alone. It was greener in Oakdale, a bit cooler, too. The longer he'd traveled, the farther he'd gotten from the drought that plagued their Covington farm. Pa had told him to go and find work after the drought had taken their wheat.

He'd hoped he'd find a job in Ashland, but everyone

there had turned him away. He'd tried again once he'd reached Greenville. In that town, it had been more of the same.

It was cooler here, but not by much. The boy wiped his face with his sleeve.

The oak tree blazed red in the last rays of sun. The boy leaned back against its trunk, letting his body rest. He was fifteen years old, his family's best chance—the last chance they had to keep regularly fed.

If he didn't find work, what would happen to them?

He could try the stables nearby, the ones not far from the alley. Maybe someone there would take pity on him or at least give him a place to sleep. The boy stood, brushed the grit from his clothes. He had no other choice but to ask.

"Sorry," the man at the stables said. "I've got no work for you here."

The boy turned to go.

"Wait. Have you tried McCalls'? The farm north of town with the newly built barn? It was painted last week; you can't miss it. I've heard Mr. McCall has hired some boys to bring in his wheat."

For the first time in days, the boy dared to hope. He quickened his pace as he followed the road that led north of town.

SCHOOL ENDS EARLY

THE SCHOOLYARD WAS busy with games and chatter. Cora saw her cousin Nettie waiting for her on the school-house steps. They'd been born five days apart. For twelve years, they'd been inseparable, but they didn't always agree.

"Have you seen this yet?" Cora pulled out the notice and smoothed it flat.

Nettie's freckled brow wrinkled as she read. "Where did you get this?"

"Near Miss Moore's shop. They're all over Main Street."

"Who's Dr. Kingsbury?" Nettie said. "I've never heard that name before."

"I don't know." It was all so exciting and strange.

A crowd of boys raced by, with one waving a handbill

over his head. Cuthbert. Nettie's little brother. He had a mouthful of crooked teeth. His hair, slick with pomade, bounced in clumps as he ran. "It's mine!" Cuthbert shouted. "You can look, but no touching."

Benjamin Vogel grabbed Cuthbert's suspenders. "Just read it to us!" he said.

They huddled together, the mass of boys, panting. "All right, but stay back. Don't step on my toe. I banged it up bad and the nail's purple now." Cuthbert looked over the handbill. "It says a doctor is coming to town."

"A stranger?" Benjamin frowned.

"From where?" someone asked.

Cuthbert shrugged. "Doesn't say."

"Why's he here?" another boy wondered.

Benjamin snatched the handbill quick. "Mine now!" He hollered and on he dashed, the doctor's notice balled in his fist.

"Nettie. Come to the square with me after school." Cora knew it was best to offer suggestions, not tell Nettie straight out what she should do. Usually Nettie wouldn't agree if something wasn't her idea first. But Cora didn't want to wait for Nettie to take the lead. "Let's go see the doctor together."

Nettie's blue eyes grew serious. "We shouldn't," she said. "You know the rules."

Don't welcome strangers. It seemed silly to Cora. "Well,

I'm going, whether you come or not."

All day whispers rippled across the schoolroom, like wind in the Great Oak's leaves. Everyone wondered about the doctor—who he was, why he'd come, and what he had planned for three o'clock in the square. Mr. Ogden, usually so observant, hadn't picked up on a thing.

"Cora. Nettie," he called from his desk. "Please come with your lessons."

Cora scooted to the end of her seat. The notice crinkled in her pocket—a reminder of Dr. Kingsbury.

Nettie's skirts swished as she walked to the front, a blond braid hanging down her back.

"Girls." Mr. Ogden nodded once they reached his desk. Usually he was clean-shaven, but today whiskers covered his cheeks. The skin under his eyes was puffy, as though he hadn't slept.

Mr. Ogden was kind to his students and generous with his time. He wasn't old, not like their last teacher. Mr. Brewster's forehead had wrinkled in an intricate map of rivers and roads, ditches and paths. But Mr. Ogden was young enough to re-member his years as a student at Oakdale School. He spoke of books he'd cherished as a boy and games he'd played in the yard. He taught arithmetic with a jar of beans and used music to explain geography. He took the whole school on nature walks and mixed paint for art lessons, never minding the flecks of color that splattered on the floor.

But in the weeks since the school term had started, Mr. Ogden hadn't been like himself. He left papers strewn across his desk instead of in his usual tidy stacks. He asked questions of the class, then startled when an answer came. And the lessons were like the ones Mr. Brewster had taught—dull and silent, except for the scratch of pencils, the flick of a turning page.

Mr. Ogden rubbed his eyes. "Which one of you will begin?"

Cora and Nettie glanced at each other. Neither had done much of their work. Before Cora could speak, Nettie started in. "I haven't been able to finish my lessons."

"And why's that? You've had all afternoon to do your work."

"The boys won't stop whispering. Cuthbert's been the worst. He busted his toe last night in the kitchen, and he wants to tell everyone how ugly it is."

"You brother's behavior isn't your concern, Miss James." Mr. Ogden turned to Cora. "Let's start with you, then."

"I'm sorry," she said, "but I haven't done much on account of Dr. Kingsbury."

Mr. Ogden's hand twitched. "Dr. Kingsbury?"

"Haven't you heard?" Nettie asked. "He's a doctor who's come to town. He claims he can cure all kinds of illnesses. Cora's got a handbill that explains everything." Nettie tugged the notice from Cora's pocket.

Cora let herself hope that Nettie had warmed to the news of the doctor. Maybe, after school, she'd come with her to his meeting.

Nettie handed the notice to their teacher. "See?"

A strange expression came over him as he read through the page.

"Mr. Ogden?" Cora said. "Are you all right?" Her eyes met Nettie's again.

He ran a hand over his head, making his hair stand on end. "What was that?"

"Should we go back to our seats? Keep on with our lessons?"

"You're excused. You and Nettie." He looked disheveled. Unkempt. "Better yet." Mr. Ogden raised his voice loud enough the whole room could hear. "All of you. School is dismissed for the day."

Books slammed shut. Slates clattered. A whoop of joy erupted in the back.

Mr. Ogden made for the door.

"What's happened to him?" Cora whispered to Nettie.

"Maybe he wants to see the doctor."

Already seats were emptying.

"Will you come with me?" Cora asked.

For a moment, Nettie hesitated. Then she slipped her arm through Cora's. "We'd better hurry if we want a good spot."

A VAGUE RECOLLECTION

FEATHERS AND FLOWERS. Ribbons and lace. What did any of it matter?

Miss Moore pushed everything aside and rested her cheek on the countertop. Her temples pulsed with pain. It was already Friday afternoon. She didn't have time for one of her headaches.

Not today.

She'd promised Mrs. Wells a new hat by tomorrow. Red ribbons with an upturned brim and a jaunty bit of frippery for decoration. Yet Miss Moore's head was so bad, she couldn't remember what would flatter the sweep of the woman's hair, the particular shape of her face.

For days she'd worked to get the hat done. Today, to buy

herself time, she hadn't opened the shop. It was a risk, with business so slow, but what other choice did she have? She'd studied her copy of *Godey's Lady's Book*—four years old and terribly out of date, but an industrious woman used what was at hand. All she had to show for her work were some sketches. A pile of ribbon. A snarl of wire. Miss Moore had barely begun.

Her temples throbbed beneath her thumbs. She pressed against the ache.

She'd do it. She'd finish. Perhaps the hat wouldn't be her best, but good enough to please the Reverend's wife. *Set your mind on the things that are above,* Reverend Wells had preached last week. Surely heavenly thoughts didn't include flowers or frills.

If only this headache would go away.

Some fresh air might help to settle the pain. Miss Moore left her stool and went to the window. Voices drifted in as she lifted the latch. Outside was the same unbearable heat. What nonsense this weather was! It worsened the pounding in her head and made it harder to concentrate. When she wrote home to Indiana next, she'd ask Mother if they'd had any rain.

The voices grew louder. What was going on? Sunlight pierced Miss Moore's eyes as she pushed the door open. It doubled the pounding in her head. She hadn't ventured out all day. That was the advantage of living in the room over her shop. One quick trip up the back stairs was all it took to reach it. But sometimes it meant she went for days without remembering to step outside.

A crowd had gathered in the square, under the shade of the old oak tree. Was it a holiday she'd forgotten? A parade to honor Oakdale's founder? This town had so many celebrations, she couldn't keep track of them.

Miss Moore didn't mix with the people here. She'd tried at first—four years ago, when she'd first come to town to care for her aunt—but no one had been very friendly. They'd nodded at her when she passed on the street but never engaged her in conversation. Once she'd invited Doris Green to take a walk in the square, but Doris had told her she wouldn't. How rude she had been! To this day, Miss Moore couldn't believe it.

But she hadn't had time to dwell on it then. In seven quick months, Aunt Matilda's cough had turned to consumption. Her aunt, once vibrant, could no longer work. Good had come of it, though. Miss Moore had learned the millinery trade. She'd inherited the shop when Matilda passed on.

Still this town wasn't home; it never would be. As soon as she'd saved enough money, she'd sell the shop here and open a new one in Indiana. Back home. Where she belonged. But business had been awful for months. Sometimes she worried she'd never leave.

A rumble came from down the road. Miss Moore

shielded her face from the sun. From a cloud of dust, a speck took shape. A chestnut mare strained in its harness. It pulled a red wagon with smooth lacquered sides. The man driving was all elbows and knees. He wore a coat as deep as death. As the man drew closer, she was able to see the slant of his nose with its crooked twist, the harsh line of his chin.

Who he was, Miss Moore didn't know. Why the crowd waited, she could only guess. Through the blur of her headache she was certain of this: She had seen the man somewhere before.

DR. KINGSBURY'S MEDICINE SHOW

THE DUST THAT hovered in the sky slowly plumed toward Main Street. Cora squeezed past Mrs. Wells, who held little Annie. She dodged Mr. Graham's crutch where it jutted out near her feet. From the dust emerged a ruddy mare pulling a peculiar wagon. Harness bells jingled with the mare's every step.

All conversation faded away. The air held the same hush as when a firecracker burns seconds before its deafening pop.

He was finally here. Dr. Kingsbury.

"There you are," Nettie said. Wisps of blond hair had slipped from her braid. "I didn't know where you'd gone."

In the crush of the crowd, in the building excitement,

Cora had forgotten her cousin. She'd pushed ahead, leaving Nettie behind. She looped her arm through Nettie's again. "Look," Cora said. "It's the doctor."

Atop the wagon was a man, thin and lanky. Dark hair brushed his shoulders. A flicker of red trimmed his coat. He had to be blazing in this awful heat. He drove from the road through the square's withered grass and stopped not far from the oak. A few people rushed forward, but most in the crowd hung back.

"Welcome, people of Oakdale!" he shouted, as though he wasn't a stranger but was here to play host.

Cora whispered to Nettie, "Let's get close as we can." They skirted the crowd, drawing near to the front.

"There's a place," Nettie said. "Near Mr. Mueller."

They squeezed in beside the red-bearded man. He nodded to them in greeting. Mr. Mueller owned the furniture shop a few doors from Father's store. His shoulders slumped forward from the hours he spent making tables and beds and his specialty, maple rocking chairs.

Near the wagon stood a boy dressed in olive and gray. Jagged brown hair hung limp on his forehead. His face narrowed to a sharp chin. When the man signaled, the boy lifted a latch. The wagon's side opened like a book laid flat. Inside was a cupboard holding rows of bottles, which glinted in the afternoon sun.

The man addressed the crowd. "My name is Dr. Elijah

Kingsbury." His tone was deep, as rich as honey.

Doctor. The word invoked a kindly old man with tinctures and pills in a small valise, not this odd-looking man and his curious wagon. Dr. Kingsbury was more than Cora had imagined, one hundred times more interesting. She didn't have to strain to catch sight of him. He knew where to stand so the whole crowd could see.

"It will happen to all, some sooner than others. The moment before your spirit takes flight, when you draw your final breath."

The crowd stirred as his words echoed in the silence.

"When the bony hand of death enters your name on the last page of the book of the living."

No one except Reverend Wells ever dared speak so boldly. It wasn't the way things were done. A thrill ran through Cora at the danger of it.

"The young and the old. Children and their elders. We aren't immune, not one of us. The cold days of winter whisper of death, as does the silence of night. Watch and take care. Death is coming!"

Cora loosened her grip on Nettie's arm. Dr. Kingsbury's meaning was both fearsome and clear. Death lurked everywhere. How had she never noticed before? It clung to the Great Oak's reddened leaves. It followed the sparrow in flight. It waited for everyone, even Cora herself.

"Death." The doctor's voiced boomed. "Who are we to try and cheat it? Every day it creeps nearer. Who can escape its skeletal grip?"

"Mama!" a child called out. Her muffled cries turned to sobs.

Dr. Kingsbury paused, searching the crowd for the child.

"Hush now," Mrs. Wells said. She scooped up Annie, who was no more than three. Annie buried her face in her mother's shoulder.

The doctor drew toward the girl. "All will be well. I promise you."

Annie lifted her head. Tears wet her lashes.

"Death is ever present, but there's no need to fear." He unpinned the bit of red on his jacket and offered it to the girl. It was a poppy, as fresh as one newly picked, though all wildflowers Cora had seen had long ago withered to brown.

"Say thank you, dear," Mrs. Wells said.

Annie played with the flower, spinning its stem.

Cora's own mother would never approve of a man who spoke freely of death and illness. It wasn't proper or very polite. There was no reason to worry that Mother was there, but still Cora found herself looking.

The doctor patted Annie's head and turned to the crowd. "While there's no way to cheat death, there is something that can hold it back. This something sustains. It shores up weakness and eliminates pain. It smooths the rough roads we all must walk and eases worldly sorrow."

Dr. Kingsbury motioned to the boy. He brought the doctor a bottle. It was made of brown glass and was stopped with a cork. The doctor lifted the bottle high. "Behold! My miraculous tonic. It relieves every malady known to man or beast."

Every malady. Every illness. How could that be?

"What about rheumatism? Does your tonic fix that?" someone shouted from the crowd.

Then voices came from all around. "Does it work on a baby with croup?"

"I've got a bum knee. Would the tonic help?"

"How about a nasty rash?"

Nearby, Mr. Ogden silently watched. His untamed hair was now slicked back. The faraway look had left his face. Cora hadn't seen him so eager in weeks.

"Yes," Dr. Kingsbury said. "My tonic would help all of those things. In twelve years of work, there've been cures in every town where I've stopped. Long before that, the tonic cured me." He took a spoon from his pocket. "When I was young, I suffered from weakness and pain in my legs. My mother said it came from growing too quickly."

He was awfully tall—long and straight as a telegraph

pole. Cora guessed he could probably reach the top shelves in Father's store with no ladder.

Dr. Kingsbury uncorked the bottle and poured the liquid into the spoon. "I used rubs to increase my circulation, applied poultices to draw out poisons, and drank my mother's strengthening tea. When none of those worked, I dedicated a year of my life to discovering a cure. It was in studying herbs I found the mixture that finally restored my vitality."

Dr. Kingsbury lifted the spoon. "My pain disappeared. I was as strong as any young man, more vigorous than I'd ever been. It wasn't long before others noticed. They asked if they might try my herbs, which I'd since made into a tonic. These people saw improvements, too. Renewed stamina. The easing of pain. Worries lessened and heartaches allayed. I knew I'd found my life's purpose—to bring relief to the suffering."

"What's it made of?" someone near the front asked.

"Mostly herbs you probably have in your cupboards and a few others you don't." He smiled. "I can't give away all of my secrets."

Dr. Kingsbury swallowed the spoonful of medicine. "I have one dose in the morning, a second in the afternoon. I'm as robust now as when I first took it." He wiped the back of the spoon on his trousers and slid it into his pocket. "But you shouldn't rely on my account. It's seeing that will help you believe. Here, let me demonstrate. Surely some of you have tender throats or a cough from the dust in the air?"

Voices murmured. Some in the crowd nodded their heads.

"I need three of you," Dr. Kingsbury said, "willing to volunteer."

The crowd grew silent. At first no one moved. Then Benjamin Vogel walked to the front, the doctor's notice still clenched in his hand. Miss Green came next, a tidy straw bonnet perched on her head. She turned to look back at the crowd, as though checking for their approval.

"Anyone else who longs for relief?"

No one made a sound.

"All right." The doctor stood between them, tall and spindly, an odd contrast in his stark black suit. "You've made a good decision, the two of you. Thank you for your willingness, Miss . . . ?"

"Green. Doris Green." She lifted her chin to meet his gaze.

"And Benjamin!" the boy blurted.

The crowd tittered. Cora tried not to laugh.

"Well, Miss Green and Benjamin. Tell me how the dust affects you."

"I wake up each morning with a raw throat," Miss

40

Green said. "Sometimes water helps, but the pain often lasts till the afternoon."

"Does it bother you now?"

She nodded.

"My throat's sore, too," Benjamin said. "And sometimes the dust makes me cough."

"Here. Have a spoonful." The doctor poured out some tonic and offered it to Miss Green. She swallowed it down and dabbed her mouth with a handkerchief.

"Benjamin, here's one for you." The boy grimaced as he took his dose.

"How's it taste?" Cuthbert shouted from somewhere in the crowd.

Benjamin puckered. "Like a bowlful of lemons."

Dr. Kingsbury turned to Miss Green. "How does it make you feel?"

"It stings a bit," she said.

"That's the medicine doing its work. Come evening, you won't even remember the pain. Any urge to cough will be gone."

"Come evening," Mr. Mueller scoffed. He crossed his arms, his broad shoulders sloping. "How easy to say they'll feel better later. By then, the show will be over, and this doctor will be long gone."

"Here's a bottle for each of you, yours to keep, in thanks

for volunteering." The doctor motioned for them to rejoin the crowd. "As I said, it can take time for the tonic to work, but sometimes a cure comes immediately. The stool, Jack," he called to his assistant.

The boy near the wagon looked uncertain. Then he fetched a small seat and set it next to the doctor.

"Is there anyone who is hard of hearing?" Dr. Kingsbury said.

There certainly was. Mr. Kennedy. The colored man owned the sawmill in town and served as city council-man. Mr. Kennedy's hearing had gotten so bad, he no lon-ger bothered trying to listen. Instead he asked people to write on the slate he wore around his neck. Most everyone obliged, except Mrs. Kennedy, who insisted shouting was quicker. It was impossible to miss their loud conversation as they entered the church or walked down the street.

A man called out, "George! Give it a try." Mrs. Ken-nedy patted her husband's shoulder and pointed to where the doctor stood.

Mr. Kennedy moved through the crowd, a brown hand steadying the slate on its string.

He was frailer than Cora remembered. Not the lumber-man she'd known her whole life, with sawdust coating his arms and his never-ending pocket of peppermints, but a bent old man in a shabby vest.

"Here," Dr. Kingsbury said, "take a seat."

Mr. Kennedy squinted. "What was that?"

The doctor repeated it, touching the stool.

"This ear of mine hasn't worked right for ages," Mr. Kennedy said. "My wife blames the rattle and clank of the mill. Says it's snatched away some of my hearing."

"My tonic will help to restore what you've lost." The doctor uncorked the bottle and instructed Mr. Kennedy to tilt his head. He poured a few drops in the man's ear.

Mr. Mueller huffed. "It'll take more than some special tonic to give George back his hearing."

Perhaps others held Mr. Mueller's opinion, but most in the crowd pressed closer in, waiting to see what would happen.

A minute passed, maybe more. All the while Mr. Kennedy kept his head at an angle. Then Dr. Kingsbury took a handkerchief and rubbed the lumberman's ear. Cora could see the doctor's lips move as he bent over Mr. Kennedy.

"Do you think it will work?" Nettie asked.

Mr. Mueller shook his head, but Cora's pulse quickened.

A permanent furrow had formed long ago on Mr. Kennedy's brow. But as Dr. Kingsbury spoke to him, that furrow eased. His eyes widened. "I hear you! I do!" Mr. Kennedy touched his ear, as though to remember the shape of it.

"Jack," the doctor called to the boy near the wagon.

"Say something to Mr. Kennedy. Let's see if he can hear you from there."

"Hello, Mr. Kennedy," the boy said. "Is it hot enough out here for you?"

"I'll say it is. Hallelujah!" Mr. Kennedy shouted. "Glory be! Thank you, Doctor. Thank you ever so much." He grabbed the doctor's hand and pumped it up and down.

The people erupted in applause.

Mr. Kennedy moved through the crowd, his back straight, his footsteps firm. Cora couldn't believe the change in him. In front of everyone Mrs. Kennedy kissed him, right on the lips.

Dr. Kingsbury recorked the tonic. "For twenty-five cents, anyone can experience the same kind of relief. Take the tonic to calm anxious nerves or to build vigor in a mind that's grown dull. Use it to remove spots on the skin or to aid any stomach complaint. Add it to the water of a horse that's grown stubborn or a dog that suffers from fleas. Start with one teaspoon in the morning, then build to a second in the afternoon."

"How long does a person have to take it?" Mrs. Wells fanned herself with a handkerchief. In her arms, Annie twisted the doctor's poppy.

"Some experience immediate change, like Mr. Kennedy. For others, they might need a few doses. I can't imagine I'll ever stop taking it."

Beside Cora, Mr. Mueller spoke. "You restored George's hearing, I'll give you that. But who's to say the rest of it's true? How could one tonic do all that you claim?"

"That's a good question," the doctor said, "one fair to ask."

"I wasn't sure of the doctor's claims, either." Cora's uncle Nathanael left the shade of the oak and offered his hand to Dr. Kingsbury. "It's good to see you again."

Nettie's braid flew as she turned to Cora. "Papa knows Dr. Kingsbury? How?"

"The doctor and I met this morning," Uncle Nathanael told the crowd. "I wasn't sure I could trust what he said until I heard this child speak." He motioned to the doctor's boy, the one called Jack.

The boy lowered his head.

Dr. Kingsbury smiled. "My assistant knows well of the tonic's power. In fact, today, for the very first time, he'll tell his own story. Now's as good a time as any. Go ahead, Jack."

The crowd, already silent, somehow grew more still.

"How convenient he's a boy from somewhere else," Mr. Mueller said. "No one here will know if he's lying."

Jack stayed where he was, near the back of the wagon. He didn't look ready or willing.

The doctor motioned Jack to come forward.

"We can't see him," someone called from the crowd.

"Let's have you stand taller, then." Dr. Kingsbury helped

him up on the stool. The tips of his dusty boots hung over its edges. Cora guessed the boy was close to her age, but balanced up there, all alone, he looked like a little kid.

Jack pushed the damp hair from his forehead.

"My sister. Lucy."

His voice was thin.

"Go on," said the doctor, "a little louder."

"My sister Lucy was sick."

The boy glanced at Annie as she spun the poppy, content in her mother's arms.

"Yes, and then what happened?" There was an edge of impatience in the doctor's question.

"And then."

Jack's cheeks blossomed red. He shut his eyes. The silence stretched uncomfortably long.

"I can't—"

Jack swayed. The stool shifted.

"Watch the boy!" Mrs. Wells shouted.

The stool slipped from under his feet. The doctor reached for Jack's arm, but too late. Jack fell, striking his head on the cupboard door. It slammed against the wagon, sending most of the bottles crashing below.

Jack pushed himself up. Put his hand to his face. Blood dripped from his fingers. Shards of glass lay on the ground. A musty scent tinged with lemon wafted through the air.

The crowd shifted and moved like a living thing.

"It's the heat," Mrs. Wells said. "Give the child some room."

"The boy was scared." Mr. Mueller shook his head. "Bet that doctor put him up to it."

Someone shouted from the back. "Give him some of your medicine, why don't you? Won't that fix him up quick?"

Pockets of laughter sprang up in the crowd.

"Not sure how he helped George Kennedy," a woman behind Cora said. "But I can't trust a man like that, a man I've never met before."

"A good show. A bit of entertainment. That's all it was," someone else muttered.

"Twenty-five cents each," Dr. Kingsbury called out, though most of the bottles had shattered. "That's nothing compared to the change you'll see." He said more, but it was impossible to catch as the crowd broke apart and drifted away.

Jack disappeared inside the wagon, the tail of his shirt pressed to his cheek. The doctor slammed the cupboard door and climbed to the top of the wagon.

That was it? He was going?

"I'd better get home," Nettie said. "Maybe I'll see you tomorrow."

Cora nodded, hardly paying attention.

Dr. Kingsbury flicked the horse's reins. The wagon wheels stirred the dust on the road. It had all been so wonderfully strange. Tonight, after supper, she'd write it down in the journal Nana had given her.

"The doctor's not done here. A fellow like him always comes back."

In the place where Mr. Mueller had been was a man Cora had never seen. Hay clung to the sleeves of his checkered shirt. A silvery beard grew from his cheeks.

"I've seen his sort before," the man said.

Gray hair snaked past his ears. What color his eyes were, she couldn't tell. They shone like a sun-brightened windowpane. Cora caught the scent of woodsmoke and grime. The old man wasn't quite clean.

"That doctor came with a task. Won't leave here until he's finished."

LISTEN AND OBSERVE

IT WAS DARK in the wagon, the air heavy and stagnant. Jack rested his forehead on his knees. The tonic bottles that hadn't broken clinked in their empty shelving. He tried to focus on the whirr of the wheels, not the unsettled feeling inside him.

The show had ended in disaster, and he was the one to blame.

He'd climbed on the stool, the whole crowd staring, and ruined everything.

Jack let his breath out slowly. Dr. Kingsbury wouldn't be pleased.

The wagon eased from the road and onto the grass. Would he be in trouble for hiding, for dashing inside the wagon alone? Sunlight cut across the wall as the doctor opened the door. He'd taken off his long black coat. The cuffs of his shirt, always so neat, were now sodden and dingy. "What was that? What happened back there?"

Dr. Kingsbury meant more than the fall. He wanted answers for Jack's hesitation. That long stretch of silence when he hadn't spoken.

"I'm not certain," Jack said.

The doctor struck a match and lit the candles on his desk. "You know what I used to tell Isaac. Once you have the crowd's attention, you must hold it as long as you can. One pause, one moment of doubt, and you've broken your bond with the audience. Do that, and no one buys tonic."

"I'm sorry. I couldn't keep my balance." The excuse sounded feeble, even to Jack. He'd never be as good at this as Isaac.

"I gave you one simple duty," Dr. Kingsbury said. "Tell your sister's story. That's all I asked. Come, let me see what you've done to yourself." Dr. Kingsbury lifted Jack's chin. "There's a lot of blood, but the cut isn't deep." He took a bottle from his pocket and soaked his handkerchief with tonic. The medicine burned as he wiped Jack's cheek. "There, that's not so bad, is it?"

"No." Jack answered, but it was a lie. He tried to hold still as Dr. Kingsbury dabbed his face.

"I don't need to remind you the money is gone.

We might have lost our chance in this town. A mistake like you've made could mean we're finished." Dr. Kingsbury pushed Jack's chin higher, hard enough his teeth clamped together uncomfortably. His thumb pressed the soft flesh not protected by bone. Jack tried to keep from wincing.

"Without any money, we have to stay put, until we're on our feet again. Tomorrow you'll spend the day in town. Your job is to learn as much as you can—whose father suffers from rheumatism, whose child struggles at school. Which family has influence, which family keeps secrets. You'll listen and observe. And since Isaac never did as I asked, you'll study the stones in the graveyard, too."

Jack caught his breath as the doctor pressed harder, the pain intentional. A memory came sharp and swift. In the grove.

Isaac had accused the doctor of something.

"Don't you forget this, Jack."

He tried to nod, but the doctor held firm. What Isaac had said angered the doctor, enough for him to hit Isaac.

He'd promised to meet Jack at the river. But the doctor said Isaac had run with the money.

"No doubt there are some who now question my claims. You have to convince them I'm someone to trust. If you do your job right, they'll seek me out. They'll come to buy the tonic."

Dr. Kingsbury blew out the candles and opened the

door. "Now go rinse your shirt and wash your face. You must look your best tomorrow."

Jack touched the tender spot under his chin. The doctor had never hurt him before. He thought of Isaac, of the doctor's mistreatment.

Cold fear spread through his body. What if the story about Isaac leaving wasn't entirely true?

A LAST CHANCE

THE BOY KNOCKED at the farmhouse door. It creaked as it opened no more than a crack.

"What do you want?" the man inside said, shadows obscuring his face.

"Mr. McCall? I heard you're hiring boys to help bring in your wheat."

"I was," McCall said, "picked up three from town. Ain't in need of any more."

The door started to close.

"Wait." The boy pushed against it. He couldn't lose this chance. "I work hard," he said. "I grew up on a farm. I won't be any trouble."

Mr. McCall didn't shut the door, but he didn't open it wider. "I told you. I don't need more help."

Night would fall soon. The boy needed a place to sleep. Yesterday, he'd eaten the last of his bread. "You could pay me less. Half of what you're giving the others."

Mr. McCall moved behind the door. "Why would I take you on? I've known them boys I hired since they were little. I've never seen you before."

"Because." The truth was all the boy had. "Back home there's a drought. It's taken most of our wheat. My pa's got a no-good hand and can't do much work on his own. My family's relying on me."

"Where you from?"

"Covington."

"You come on your own?"

"Yes," the boy said.

Silence filled the gloom. Soon night would dress the sky in stars. The boy thought it was over. He turned to leave.

"I suppose I could give you a trial run. But don't think half the pay means half of the work. You'll need to eat, too. I'd dock that from your wages."

"Thank you so much. I promise, you won't be disappointed."

"I'll be the judge of that." The door opened wider. Mr. McCall offered his hand. "What's your name, son?"

"Silas. Silas Carey."

"Well, Silas Carey, don't get too excited. I take nothing less than good, honest effort. You'll have to prove your worth. For now, go make a bed in the hayloft. Be up early. Work starts with the sun."

UNWELCOME

"WATCH IT, BOY," a man growled. "You can't just stand there gawking about."

Jack stepped from the sidewalk to get out of the way.

Yesterday morning when he'd come to town, he'd only seen the old dog. Now all kinds of people bustled about in the mid-morning heat. Boots thumped the sidewalks. Wagons crowded the streets. Shop doors fluttered like birds testing their wings.

What was Jack supposed to say to this town full of strangers?

He kept to the road, trying to pretend he'd come on an errand, like he'd done back home for Ma.

From inside the bakery, a boot nudged the door open. A

woman in gray with a basket of loaves struggled to squeeze through.

"Do you need help?" His words sounded small, like the cries of a kitten.

The woman braced the door, a stony expression on her face. "I don't," she said. "Not from you."

Jack touched his cheek. Had the fall made him bruise? He didn't think there was blood on his skin. Yesterday he'd washed as well as he could, but the doctor had no mirror. Jack knew his shirt wasn't dirty. He'd taken care scrubbing until the water ran clean. But these reassurances didn't mean anything. She must have seen the flop that was yesterday's show.

From inside, someone pulled the door wider, allowing the woman to find her way out. A boy watched from the bakery window.

Jack hurried on, his hands sunk in his pockets. It could take time for a town to warm to a stranger. He'd seen it before, but that made it no easier. The people here felt especially distant.

Not far from the bakery, several women admired the hats in the milliner's window. They drew close together as he approached, their conversation fading.

This was all wrong, like that time he'd accidentally tracked mud across the kitchen floor. Ma had scolded him, but once Jack had wiped up the mud, she'd helped him rinse the rags clean.

He'd made a mess in Oakdale, too, but no one had reason to offer him kindness.

In front of the general store, two men sat, an upturned barrel between them. A checkerboard balanced on the barrel's end jiggled with every turn. "That's three wins for me!" boasted the older man, who was seated on an apple crate. His chin disappeared into his neck like a turtle pulled into its shell. As he shot out a hand to claim the last checkers, his gaze drifted to Jack. "Well, look who's here. The doctor's boy."

Isaac's trousers felt too long, too bunched at the knees. Suspenders couldn't hide how they gaped at his waist.

The younger man stared. A few stray whiskers dotted his cheeks. "Thought you and the doctor would be long gone by now."

Jack tried to push his discomfort aside. "We're staying in the willow grove, if you know anyone looking for tonic."

The older man set up his checkers again. "Looking to throw away money, you mean?"

"The medicine's good. It's worth every penny."

The older man chuckled, saying no more.

Jack was unwanted here, as unwelcome as a spider in a sack of dry beans.

He kicked at the road as he walked on, till a fine layer of dust coated his boots. Ahead, two men balanced on ladders, one on each side of Main Street, a banner stretching between them. They lifted it high and secured it with ropes.

— CELEBRATE FOUNDER'S DAY —
SATURDAY, OCTOBER 22.
May Our Roots Sink as Deep as the Great Oak Tree.
Only ____ Days to Go.

The man on the right shifted his ladder. He attached a canvas square to the empty space. Jack read the banner again. *Only 14 Days to Go.*

Founder's Day. That was something worth telling the doctor about.

Someone jostled him as a rush of people crowded the sidewalk. The old stray crossed the empty road. As it reached the other side, the crowd fell back to the street. Were the people afraid of the dog? It wasn't diseased or infected with mites, only old and in need of a bath. Not far from the general store, it entered an alley and settled where the sun didn't reach.

"Hey, you there."

Jack raised his eyes to a ginger-haired man who carried a chair from the furniture shop. The man lifted it to the back of a wagon that waited on the street.

"Tell me, son. How'd that doctor of yours fix George's ear?"

There wasn't much Jack could say. He didn't know how the medicine worked. "He poured in some tonic and wiped off the extra. I've seen it help lots of folks." The grandmother in Greenville who'd been deaf for years. The farmer outside Covington with inflamed feet. In Greenville, the woman had cried when she'd heard her granddaughter speak. Near Covington, the doctor had bathed the man's feet while he still wore his boots. The medicine was so potent, it soaked straight through the leather. How could Jack begin to explain it?

The ginger-haired man scratched his beard. "Funny how nobody bought a bottle."

"Well," Jack said, embarrassed, "there weren't many left by the end of the show."

The man leaned against the wagon like he was settling in for a chat. "You said your sister was sick. Is it true? Or did the doctor put you up to it?"

"No," Jack said. "I would never—"

"I think there's something you're not telling me. I think your doctor's playing a trick."

"That's not true!"

"It's not?" The man smirked. "What's the truth, then?"

He'd probably seen Jack make a fool of himself—the silence, the fall, every last bit.

Jack shoved past the man and started to run. Laughter floated from the end of the road, where kids played in the square. They were probably laughing at him right now, the boy who'd bungled his words, who couldn't keep to his feet.

He only stopped running when he entered the alley. It was much cooler there, away from the sun, a safe and quiet space.

The dog lifted its head as he approached. Though its black coat was matted in places, the fur looked smooth and soft. Jack knelt and stroked the dog's ears. It nuzzled him with its nose. No, not it, Jack told himself. The dog was a he. A gentle sort. Dogs weren't like people, standoffish and wary. They were eager to offer kindness.

The old boy rolled over, exposing a freckled belly. Jack gave it a scratch. Too bad the dog couldn't talk. He probably knew Oakdale better than anyone.

If Isaac were here, people would trust him. Isaac made everyone comfortable. Without him, Oakdale had started all wrong.

Jack took a small figure from his pocket, let the dog sniff the misshapen wood. It looked more like a lump than the cat Jack imagined, a gift he'd one day give Lucy. By the time it was hers, the cat's nose would be tucked under one paw, and the tail would curve around its body till it ended at a crooked tip.

Jack wasn't good at whittling yet, but he would be, with practice.

Isaac had shown him how to follow each twist of the wood, how to discover what shape was hidden inside. He'd taught Jack how a too-deep cut could be mended and a slip of the blade could be peeled away with just a few extra strokes.

If only mistakes in real life could be managed the same. But those sorts of mistakes cut deeper than knives. Their marks often couldn't be fixed.

Jack worked on the carving long enough a ring of shavings surrounded his boots. Shadows crept down the alley's walls. His rumbling stomach told him it was probably close to noon. He wanted to stay where he was, but he couldn't hide out forever. So far he hadn't learned much. Hopefully that would change at the graveyard. Jack closed his knife and put it away. The old dog followed behind.

MR. OGDEN'S SECRET

THE DOCTOR'S BOY was still here. Mr. Ogden had seen him not far from Brindley's. If the boy was here, the doctor was too.

Mr. Ogden sat at his desk, the schoolhouse radiant with sun. He'd always loved coming in on Saturdays to prepare for the school week ahead. The empty desks. The polished wood floor. They were the same as when he'd been a boy, when he'd worked and studied and dreamed one day he'd teach in this very place.

He'd taken schools in other towns, waiting for the position in Oakdale. Three years ago, Mr. Brewster had left. That hope had finally come true. He'd relished these

Saturdays, alone in the schoolhouse, but that had changed when he'd noticed the tremor.

Mr. Ogden placed his hands in his lap and looked at the difference between them. Both hands were large with squared-off nails. His left had a callus from holding a pen. But while his right hand lay still, the left one quaked.

He'd been hiding this secret for weeks now.

He'd first noticed the shaking here at his desk as he'd written a lesson for the second-year class. As Mr. Ogden had gripped his pen, one finger had moved on its own. Small but insistent, like a nervous tic.

A few days later, he'd seen it again. That time it wasn't only his finger but his entire hand that had trembled like a man racked with worry. Then his foot had clenched as he'd left the schoolhouse, making his footsteps unfamiliar.

He was a stranger in his own body, unsure what to expect.

It reminded him of the shaking palsy, the disease that had left Mr. McCall a stooped and shuffling old man. But he, Walter Ogden, wasn't elderly, only thirty-two. How could he have the same condition as one so much older?

In the early days when he'd first seen the tremor, he'd planned to visit a doctor in Cleveland, even though it was seventy miles away. As soon as he could, he would go to the city and have an expert look after him. Then his sister had come to town on a visit and stayed for nearly two weeks.

The school board had asked that he write up a piece about Oakdale's history for Founder's Day. He'd had no chance to leave, no time that was really his own. There was no one he could confide in here, not even his parents. He'd tried doing so once or twice, but stopped when he imagined his father's concern, the anguish etched on his mother's face. It was best not to worry them. One hint that something was wrong and the news would get out and spread.

No one could suspect anything.

He squeezed his hands into fists and opened them again. While his right fingers moved as they should, the left ones stayed partially curled. He tried pushing them flat.

The teacher before him, Mr. Brewster, had been asked to step aside. Not because of his age or his teaching but because he'd developed a nagging illness. His health posed a problem, the school board said. It was better for him to go.

Mr. Ogden wouldn't let that happen to him. Teaching was the only job he'd ever wanted, the only one he was qualified for. If word got out that his body was failing, who'd offer him work, anyhow?

He sighed as he leaned back in his chair. Had anyone noticed a change in him? The shaking and stiffness only happened occasionally, yet it took so much effort to try to conceal them. He kept his hands in his pockets as much as he could. When his foot tensed, he'd stand where he was until the tightening passed.

The symptoms had kept him from so many things. Stringing beads with the little ones. Nature outings. Painting lessons. Teaching the older children how to dance the Virginia reel.

He didn't know how much longer he could keep this secret.

That was why the doctor's notice had given him hope, why that hope had been dashed when the show ended abruptly and the doctor had driven away.

But the boy was still here. That meant Dr. Kingsbury wasn't far off. Mr. Ogden would go and look for him. If the tonic did what the doctor claimed, he wouldn't need to hide his condition.

He'd be free of it once and for all.

THE GRAVEYARD

THE OLD WOODEN bench had been in the graveyard long before Cora was born. Its armrests were worn slick and shiny from use. Weathered boards sagged in its middle. She'd never seen anyone sit there, not once, though the bench was set in a welcoming spot that offered plenty of shade.

The boards creaked as she eased herself down to study the gravestone before her. Time had softened the sharp-cornered epitaph. Lichen hid letters in shades of rust. Still Cora could read the words underneath as she shielded her face from the afternoon sun.

ROBERT FRASIER

1672–1761

FOUNDER

FAITHFUL HUSBAND

FATHER

FRIEND TO ALL

✚

May His Memory Ever Thrive
Like the Great Oak Tree

Cora checked to be certain she was alone. "Hello." Her voice dropped to a whisper. "Uncle Robert." The name sounded peculiar, somehow too close and private, although she was free to use it. He was her uncle—generations back, on her mother's side.

Since Nana's memory had started to waver, Cora came to his grave for company.

She had Nettie, of course, but no one listened like Uncle Robert. Like Nana, he was never impatient. He never interrupted what she had to say. He never insisted her thoughts weren't in keeping with a girl from one of Oakdale's first families.

She moved to the edge of the bench and rested her elbows on her knees. There was so much she wanted to tell him. "Yesterday a doctor came to town. The first one ever, I think."

On the tree above, a sparrow alighted among the withered leaves. The graveyard had suffered these months without rain, yet sprigs of grass grew near the marker. Someone had cared for this part of the graveyard. Reverend Wells, perhaps.

"The doctor fixed Mr. Kennedy's ear. You should see him now! Mrs. Kennedy told me this morning he's pleased as a rooster that's seen the sun after days of rain."

Cora pressed her palm against the warm stone. "What was it like when Oakdale first started? When new people came to town? I'm not sure what to make of Dr. Kingsbury, and yesterday Mr. Mueller said—"

The sparrow called from its branch before flying off. Cora watched it sail deeper into the graveyard, past the first row of stones and—what was that? A boy. And the smelly old stray. A flutter of white gave them away, a piece of paper the boy held in his hand. He was the one from the medicine show.

Had he heard her? How embarrassing! Sometimes, when talking, she got louder and louder. At least, that's what Nettie said. Cora slumped on the bench, hoping he'd been too far away. She tried to remember his name. It started with a *J.* Maybe James or Jack? She watched as he wrote on his paper.

What was he doing exactly? She'd been coming to this graveyard her whole life. There was nothing here so important it required writing down.

Careful with strangers. They're not always trustworthy. The words came to her without any bidding. But why should she mind them? She wanted to know what the boy was doing. Cora left the bench and crept down the path to the closest row of stones. She knelt in the back so she'd stay hidden.

This part of the graveyard was shaped like a wheel, each spoke a row of whitewashed markers. The path circled the rows like a steel tire. At the center stood a woman in white, a marble statue on a high pedestal surrounded by cobblestones.

The boy entered the next row of graves. After taking some notes at the first granite marker, he moved to the second one. Cora's knees ached where they pressed the ground. How long was he going to take? She moved deeper in, toward the stone statue. If she could get a better look, she'd figure out what he was doing.

He wrote as he walked from grave to grave, every step drawing him nearer. Cora circled the statue as he reached the cobblestones, ducking behind its base.

He made his last scribble and lifted his eyes. "Oh!" he said, as he caught sight of her.

Cora slipped out of her hiding place. "Sorry. I didn't mean to surprise you."

"I didn't know anyone else was here."

The statue named Truth held her arms wide, keeping

watch over the dead as she always had. Or maybe the marble woman was Grace? Cora couldn't remember.

"What are you doing?" she asked the boy.

He hid the piece of paper behind his back. "Just looking."

"At what?"

He shrugged. "I'm doing some work."

Cora laughed. "By wandering around the headstones?"

"It's true," he said. "It's for the doctor."

That was odd—but also interesting. The boy probably did this in every town. "Why would Dr. Kingsbury want you to visit our graveyard?"

His gray eyes met hers, quickly darted away. "He says a town's present takes root in its past."

That sounded like what Mr. Ogden might say, when he was more like himself. But what could the doctor gain from the graveyard? He wasn't here for those who'd passed on but had come to heal the living.

Cora moved closer in. "Jack? That's your name, isn't it?"

He nodded.

"I'm Cora Brindley." She made sure to keep back from the stray. "You don't have to let that dog near you, you know."

Everyone knew the stray was bad luck. Sometimes Father threw the dog scraps, but even he wouldn't dare touch it. Years ago, it had wandered into town, a pup left by someone passing through. Cora was told she must never go near it. Nobody knew the dog's history. It had shown up the same day Mrs. Kennedy had lost her wedding ring. Then Mr. Mueller had tripped over it as it huddled outside his furniture shop. He'd broken his leg and was laid up for weeks.

Jack stroked the dog's grizzled head. "I like him. He's good company."

What a strange boy he was. His jagged brown hair grew well past his ears. It looked like he'd cut it without any help, when help was certainly needed. His too-big clothes were faded and worn; his eyes were the shade of granite. Jack's face narrowed to a small, pointed chin. Quiet and serious, Mother would say, from a family that didn't have much. What other kind would send him to work with a man like Dr. Kingsbury?

Jack touched the gravestone nearest him. "You have a lot of Thompsons here."

A curious boy saying curious things, but Cora had to agree. "We've got more Thompsons than any town needs. There are four at school, curly haired, every one. The twins aren't so bad, but the little ones! My teacher, Mr. Ogden, says they'll outgrow their fussing, but I don't know about that. Last week, Angelica Thompson wouldn't come in from recess. One of the twins had to carry her back. Eddie, the littlest, thought it looked like fun, like Angelica was in a parade. The next morning *he* refused to come in."

Cora stopped. She'd gotten a little off track, maybe told this boy more than was needed. How could she not help but feel excited? Jack had traveled far beyond Oakdale. He'd seen so many things! Maybe not that Chicago skyscraper or a city lit up with electrical lights, but so much more than she ever had.

Jack scribbled on his paper again. "What about the Kennedys? Wasn't Mr. Kennedy the colored man whose hearing the doctor restored?"

"Well, yes," Cora said. "But why should you get to ask all the questions?" There was plenty she wanted to know. Where was he from? Shouldn't he be in school? What was it like to live with the doctor?

She took a sack of marbles from her pocket—agates and alleys and corkscrews and clams, and even a few cat's-eyes. A couple of them Cuthbert had given her, but most she'd bought at Father's store. "I'll answer yours if you answer mine."

"All right," Jack said.

"We get five marbles each." Cora counted them out. "One marble for one question. Once your marbles are gone, your questions are finished. I'll go first." She set a marble on the cobblestone, a corkscrew with swirls of blue and red.

"Where are you from? How long have you been with the doctor?" She crossed her fingers, hoping Jack wouldn't notice she'd asked more than one question.

"I come from a farm outside Covington. I've been with the doctor for over a year."

"Have you stayed in Ohio the whole time you've traveled?"

"Mostly," Jack said. He put a marble next to Cora's. "That was three questions. You still haven't answered mine."

So that was how Jack was going to play. He was the sort to hold fast to the rules. Cora placed two marbles next to her first. "The Kennedy family came from Greenville, long before my grandmother was born. The youngest ones go to school with me." Cora knew in some towns colored families weren't welcome. Some places they couldn't own land or go to school with everyone else. "Mr. Kennedy owns the sawmill. Mrs. Kennedy takes in sewing. She makes the most beautiful dresses in town. For years, Mr. Kennedy wore a slate around his neck. He insisted people write on it, on account of his poor hearing." But not anymore, not since Dr. Kingsbury's cure.

"Next question." Cora set her fourth marble down. "Tell me about the places you've been. Where have you gone? What have you seen? Which has been your favorite so far?"

"I'm not sure," Jack said. "There have been so many. After a while it's hard to remember."

Cora couldn't believe it. If she ever had a chance like Jack, she'd take it, quick as she could. She wouldn't forget anything. But what girl could ever do that? Maybe when the doctor left town, she could hide in the back of his wagon. Not so long her family would worry, but just long enough to catch a glimpse of the world that lay beyond Oakdale.

Just for a minute, she let herself dream.

"There was one thing I saw. A lighthouse," Jack said. "A single white column with a red-tiled roof and a light that roamed the water. Standing on the edge of Lake Erie, it felt like the end of the world."

Cora imagined the wandering light, the crash of waves as the wind burned her cheeks. If only she could see something like that!

Jack placed his next marble on the cobblestones. "What do you know about the Muellers?"

"They've been in town almost from the beginning. They're one of Oakdale's first families. Old Mrs. Mueller died a few years ago. She was known for her rhubarb pies. Baked the best in the county, people said."

The dog flumped at Jack's feet, sending the marbles in every direction. Cora scooped them up and lined them again along the cobblestones.

"Mr. Mueller runs the furniture store. He makes maple rocking chairs, though you have to be careful to check them. Sometimes the ash from his pipe burns a mark on the wood. He insists it's part of the furniture's charm."

"He's got a red beard?"

Cora nodded. It was nice to have someone to talk to. Nettie wasn't always interested in everything Cora wanted to say. And as much as she liked Uncle Robert, it was good to have someone who answered her back.

"Does Dr. Kingsbury live in his wagon?" she asked.

"That's where he works. We sleep outside."

"Outside?" She said. "On the ground?"

"It's not so bad. We've got blankets, of course, and when it rains we sleep under the wagon."

She'd already reached her number of questions. Probably double that. But Cora couldn't help asking a couple more. "Where's the doctor from?"

"Pennsylvania," Jack said, "though he hasn't been there for years."

"Is he as mysterious as he seems?"

"That was a whole lot more than five questions. It's my turn now." Jack studied his sheet of paper. "What can you tell me about the Vogels?"

She had lots of stories about Benjamin Vogel. That time he dared Cuthbert to stand on his desk. How he loved the word "flapdoodle" and ate peaches with scoops of vanilla ice cream. "Benjamin Vogel's my cousin's friend. He and Cuthbert think up more mischief together than you could ever imagine." Cora pushed on with her last questions. "What's the doctor really like? After the show. When you're with him alone?"

"Nope." Jack shook his head. "You're finished." She could tell he was trying not to smile. She knew he had more to say but he wouldn't.

This boy. He was exasperating.

He opened his hand. "I'll give these three marbles back if you tell me about the tree in the square."

The Great Oak. It was the most important part of Oakdale's history. Cora knew the oak's story by heart. It was too good to keep to herself. She took the marbles from his outstretched hand. "It's a long story. Mr. Ogden, my teacher, tells it every year. We'll need somewhere comfortable to sit. Come, follow me."

She led Jack down the rows of stones to the bench under the tree.

"Oakdale's founder, Robert Frasier, was my great-great-uncle, generations back. This is where he's buried."

"Your uncle? Really?"

"Yes, and you've already met my other one. Mayor James, he's my uncle, too."

Jack scribbled on his paper again. What would he do with the things he'd written? Had she said more than she should? But no, that was silly. There was no harm in talking.

Carefully, Cora picked her words. She hoped Jack would feel the same wonder she did.

"A long time ago, Robert Frasier left home. Besides a wagon and rifle, he brought one other thing—a tree he'd nurtured from acorn to seedling. Robert bound the roots in a burlap sack and secured the tree in a pail. For weeks he traveled across miles of prairie, searching for the right piece of land."

Jack didn't move as Cora spoke. She trusted the story had drawn him in.

"The land Robert chose had to be level, but not so far from the hills that a violent wind might uproot the tree. The land needed water and a view of the skies. Once he found the perfect place, Robert planted the oak. Twice a day he hauled river water, one bucket for the sapling and one for himself. He tended that tree like he would his own child. That was almost two hundred years ago."

Cora always wondered how life would be different if he'd picked another place instead.

"It takes an oak many years to mature. But Robert Frasier claimed once the oak set its roots, its trunk broadened until it was thick as a hay bale. Food was scarce when the weather turned cold. Geese called from the skies, flying too high for his rifle. The deer and the rabbits disappeared with the snow. Even when Robert cut a hole in the ice, the fish refused to bite. He lived through the winter on piles of acorns he gathered from the tree. The oak cared for him as he'd once cared for it. That's why we fence the tree off. To keep it protected. So we always remember how our town came to be." The wrought-iron fence had circled the tree her whole life and probably long before that. "The oak reminds us how deep our roots sink. No one's to touch it, not even the Reverend when he waters it during seasons like this."

Of any dry stretch Cora remembered, these months had been the worst. There were farms not far from town that had lost both corn and wheat.

If only the rains would come soon.

Jack stroked the dog's head. "Yesterday was the first time I helped in the show. It didn't go quite as I'd hoped."

Cora never had trouble with words, but now she wasn't sure how to begin. Yesterday, on that stool, Jack had looked so small and alone.

"You said . . . ," she started. "You said your sister . . ."

"Lucy's her name."

"The tonic made Lucy better?"

Jack nodded. "She'd had a fever for weeks. Mostly she slept, though sometimes Ma could coax her to sip a little broth."

79

The stray nudged Jack with its nose, as if it knew he needed some comfort. Cora kept her eyes on the granite marker, to give Jack a moment alone.

"My ma got Lucy to swallow the tonic. By morning her fever had broken and the color had returned to her cheeks. That's why I left with the doctor. His tonic saved Lucy. He pays me each month, and I send it home. He's given my family everything."

Jack was an unexceptional boy. That's what Mother would say if she met him, a stranger who shouldn't stay longer than needed. But that's not what Cora believed. This boy had left all he'd known for the doctor. She'd never done anything half as brave.

She'd never met anyone like him.

The statue's long shadow reached over the cobblestones. Memory. That was her name. She honored those who were buried here, a reminder their lives wouldn't be forgotten.

Though it still felt like summer, the days had grown shorter. The sun would be setting soon. If Cora stayed any longer, she wouldn't make it to supper on time. "I come here a lot. If ever you're looking for someone to talk to . . ." The words sounded stupid. She bit her lip.

"I'd like that," Jack said. A dimple formed in his cheek as he smiled. "I hope I'll see you again."

LITTLE MISTAKES

THREE BOYS FROM Oakdale. Each close to his age. None of them cared for Silas.

That first day in the field, he and two others followed a boy cutting wheat with a scythe. The blade sliced through the stalks, leaving piles to bundle. Silas knew how to gather those bundles, how to bind them together with straw. No one talked as they worked, as the sun burned their fore-arms and sweat soaked their backs. When they stopped for a drink, no one answered when Silas asked their names.

The three boys looked him over with quick, darting glances. They were no more than sixteen. As they lifted their cups, they turned away. A wall of white shirts and black suspenders closed him off from their conversation.

Henry and Bill and Raymond. Silas caught their names as they talked. Henry was the one with the shock of hair the color of sun-dried wheat. Bill was the one with reddish curls. Dark-headed Ray swung the grain scythe.

All morning, Henry had played little pranks. He'd poured water for everyone, but sloshed half from the cup he handed Silas. More than once in the field, Henry kicked the pile of wheat that Silas had gathered. The pranks were so small they might have been accidents.

Little mistakes.

When they broke to eat, the three of them opened their dinner pails. They pulled out slices of bread slathered in bacon grease, apples and cheese and even some pie. Silas unwrapped what the missus had given him. One meager square of corn bread from supper the night before.

Henry swallowed the last of his bread. "The boy's wondering why we won't talk to him, when it's his job he should wonder about. Last week McCall said he was done hiring, even though my brother still needed work. I don't know how this kid convinced McCall, but he's stolen a spot from a local boy."

After that, Silas kept to himself. He worked hard enough no one could complain, doubly hard as the rest of them. He put up with silence and unfriendly stares by remembering his family at home.

The heat that had followed Silas to town grew worse as

the weeks wore on. The grass dried. The crops withered. For days on end, the clouds gathered, but they never gave any rain.

In the morning, before work started in, Silas walked the fields and watched the skies. As the gray dawn of morning welcomed the day, he found his spirits lifted. The boys didn't like him, but Mr. McCall was pleased with his work. Silas wouldn't be in Oakdale forever. He could hold on a few months more.

One of those early mornings, he saw a girl perched on a fence. The sun had just started to awaken the heavens. Eyes closed, she'd raised her face to the sky, a smile playing on her lips. "Hello," she said, as Silas approached. "Have you ever seen such a glorious day?"

The girl's name was Evangeline. She was the one bit of good he'd found in Oakdale.

A NIGGLING MEMORY

MISS MOORE SAT on a stool behind the counter, threading a needle with a crimson strand. She'd tried to finish Mrs. Wells's hat, but her work still wasn't done. She blamed the headache she'd had since yesterday morning. That and Alma James and her silly friend Doris. The two had spent most of the afternoon rummaging through her shop. Miss Moore had refolded handkerchiefs they'd muddled. She'd followed behind, tidying discarded hats.

Of course Miss Moore wanted customers, but did they have to leave such a mess?

"I can't understand why that child's still here." Alma James turned, watching her reflection, a gingham-ribboned bonnet atop her head. She had arched brows and a graceful neck, like that sister of hers, Lauren Brindley. "No, this one doesn't suit me, either." She loosened the ribbons tied under her chin.

If Alma was a precious stone, Doris was plain as a pebble.

"The boy should be in school," Doris said.

Alma set the bonnet on its stand, its brim crooked and ribbons rumpled.

Miss Moore sighed. Couldn't they take better care? She squeezed between the two women and set the bonnet right again. Surely, if they planned on making a purchase, they would have done so by now.

Doris touched another hat's feathered brim. "What was his mother thinking? If he were my child, I'd never let him travel the country with a man like that."

A man like that doctor person, she meant. Since he'd ridden into town in his red lacquered wagon, Eloise Moore couldn't shake the conviction that she'd seen him somewhere before. She'd spoken with him, too; she knew it. As soon as he started that gruesome speech, Miss Moore had remembered his voice.

It wasn't in Oakdale she'd heard him speak. It was some other place.

But where?

At home in Indiana, she'd never been to a medicine show. Her family's only doctor visit was when they'd all had the mumps. An old man had come to assist them that day, not the dark-haired man with his tonic.

This man. This Dr. Kingsbury. When had she met him before?

Miss Moore shut her eyes to remember. There had been a large crowd. A silvery flash, like the sun striking a shovel's blade. Or perhaps it had been the gleam of a flute. Or the glimmer of polished stone. The memory was no more than a shadow. Yet she knew when she'd first seen him, the man who called himself Dr. Kingsbury had been no doctor at all.

"Excuse me, Miss Moore." Alma James held a felt hat, a silk rose stitched to the brim. It didn't suit her, not in the least. "Might you make one like this with a red rose instead? I'd like to be able to pick it up the Tuesday after next."

She'd wear a felt hat in this horrible heat? And a red rose she wanted, when pink most flattered the hat's soft colors. Miss Moore opened her ledger to make note of the date. "I could do that, Mrs. . . . ?"

"Please call me Alma. Alma James."

Of course she knew this was Alma James, wife to the mayor and head of the Ladies' Auxiliary. But the name Alma was too familiar. Mrs. James was sufficient. It was simple and clear. A given name was an invitation, a possibility that with time and charity, an acquaintance might turn into a friend.

Miss Moore glanced at Doris Green, fidgeting with a hat on its stand. She remembered the snub from four years ago. Miss Moore could still feel its sting. People in Oakdale didn't like strangers. That was something she'd figured out quickly. By the time a few of them warmed to her, she'd already moved on.

Thankfully, she wouldn't be here much longer. A few months more, and she'd have enough money—if everything kept to the schedule she'd made.

"I'm buying the hat for the Auxiliary Tea," Alma James said. "Are you planning on coming this year?"

"Not this time, I'm afraid." Hardly a month passed without some invitation, always from Alma James. How long must she refuse before Mrs. James realized she never planned to attend?

Doris came to the counter, a bonnet in hand. "Alma, I heard the doctor and his assistant are staying in the grove. You know how his tonic soothed my throat. There's a chance it might help Nettie's blemishes."

"Goodness." Mrs. James's cheeks reddened. "I'd rather not discuss my daughter's complexion."

"Even so. If he's still in town, there's no harm in asking." Doris placed the bonnet on the countertop. "I'll need a hatbox for this." She didn't even bother to look at Miss Moore.

The snub was as clear as it had been before, when Doris

declined Miss Moore's invitation to go for a walk in the square. "Give me one moment." Miss Moore took her time reaching the back of the shop. She studied the hatboxes stacked on the shelves and picked the one that was hardest to reach.

That Doris could stand the wait.

But Miss Moore also needed to think, and the delay gave her opportunity. If she'd seen Dr. Kingsbury in Indiana, that meant it had been at least four years past. In his show, Dr. Kingsbury claimed he'd sold medicine for, what was it? Ten years? No. Not ten. He'd said twelve. Yet her memory told her otherwise.

She needed to see him again, hear the man speak. That might trigger the memory.

Miss Moore returned with the box. She settled the hat inside. "I don't mean to hurry you out, but I plan on closing soon."

That was exactly what she meant, no two ways about it.

There was a hat she needed to finish, the headache that wouldn't let her be, and a niggling memory she must put to rest.

Alma and Doris gathered their things. Miss Moore flipped the sign that hung in the window. From the road, all would see she'd closed for the day. "Goodbye now," she said as she held the door open and Alma and Doris left the shop.

FIVE PENNIES

AS JACK TOOK the path into the grove, he tried to re-member what Cora had said. One woman sewed dresses. Another baked pies. The red-bearded man made rocking chairs. Mueller. Wasn't that his name? And then there had been that incredible story she'd told about the tree.

How lucky Jack had been to meet Cora. He'd taken his time walking the graveyard, unsure what he was looking for. What information did the doctor want? Jack couldn't tell. That's why Cora had been such a help. Surely something he'd written down would interest Dr. Kingsbury.

Jack slowed when he heard voices ahead.

"There's no reason to worry, Mr. . . ."

"Ogden. Walter Ogden."

Cora had mentioned a Mr. Ogden. Jack ducked behind a screen of willows and looked over the notes he'd taken. Mr. Ogden was her teacher. He must have seen Jack while he was in town.

"Your secret stays with me."

Not everyone wanted their hardships known. Some sought out the doctor privately. Jack pulled the willow branches aside, his curiosity getting the better of him.

In the clearing the man talked with Dr. Kingsbury. He held a sack in the crook of his arm.

"I can't control my fingers. They move on their own," Mr. Ogden was saying. He held out his hand in front of the doctor. His finger and thumb shifted together, as though he were rolling a small object between them, but from what Jack could see, nothing was there. "It's the same with my foot. One minute it's fine, then my muscles stiffen, making it hard to move properly. I've started taking my exercise early so no one will see." He clasped his trembling hand with the other. "I think it might be the palsy."

"Palsy hardly ever strikes a man your age. It's rare but not unheard-of."

"Will your tonic help, do you think?"

"It will," Dr. Kingsbury said, "though you won't see change immediately. A tonic takes time to build up in the body. It could be a number of days, even weeks, before you see a difference."

A few weeks? Jack had never heard the doctor say that. He'd always insisted the tonic worked quickly, just as it had for Lucy. A couple of doses was all it took, if it didn't help straightaway.

"How many bottles may I interest you in?"

Don't leave a customer, Isaac once said. *When you're close to a sale, don't give him a chance to change his mind.* The wagon, set back under the trees, was a good distance from where the two men stood. Jack left his hiding place. He needed to fetch the tonic.

"There you are," the doctor said, "and not a moment too soon."

Jack didn't have to be told what to do. He opened the cupboard door.

"Four bottles," Mr. Ogden said. "No, wait. Make that five. I want to be sure I've got enough."

There were six bottles of tonic that hadn't broken. Jack took them all, in case Mr. Ogden wanted one more.

"I've brought an extra, if you'd like."

"Thank you, Jack. That's your name, isn't it?" Mr. Ogden put them in his sack and set it on the ground.

"Take your first spoonful as soon as you're home," Dr. Kingsbury said. "Then keep to that dose for the next seven days. If the palsy remains after a week, add a second spoonful in the afternoon. Don't be discouraged if it takes a while. If you need more, I'll be in the grove."

Why would Mr. Ogden need more tonic? He'd already bought all that was left. But the doctor knew best. There had to be a good reason.

"How long do you plan to stay in Oakdale?"

"A few weeks," Dr. Kingsbury said. "I suspect we'll be gone by the middle of October."

"Are you waiting on the other boy?"

"Other boy?" The doctor paused, his jaw tightening. "I'm not sure what you mean."

"Your other assistant. The older one. I saw him yesterday morning. When he wasn't at the medicine show, I thought perhaps the older boy had—"

The doctor cut in. "There's no other boy. You're mistaken."

"Really?" Mr. Ogden's brow wrinkled. "I suppose it could have been someone from town. When I opened the schoolhouse, I was quite certain—" He shook his head. "No matter. My mind has been jumbled." The bottles clinked as he picked up the sack. "Thank you, Dr. Kingsbury. I'm sure we'll see each other again. If not here, then in town."

The sun, golden now, bathed the grove in evening light. A peculiar feeling settled in Jack's chest as he watched the man go. Mr. Ogden had seen Isaac. Yesterday morning, near the schoolhouse.

Dr. Kingsbury put his arm around Jack. "Well done,

bringing out that last bottle. Now that we've had one customer, there are sure to be more."

"Did you hear?" Jack's words trailed off as his thoughts caught up to his understanding. Mr. Ogden had seen Isaac, but the doctor said he had no other assistant.

"Did I hear what?"

"Nothing," Jack said.

"You're a good boy." Dr. Kingsbury smiled. "You know when to talk and when to listen." He reached into his pocket, then held out his hand, his eyes fixed on Jack. "Here. Take these extra pennies. They're yours to keep, not to send home. Spend them any way you wish."

Five pennies all his own. Jack had never had so many at once. Maybe he'd buy himself candy or a hot slice of blueberry pie.

"Go catch us some fish, and I'll start a fire. You can tell me what you learned in town once we sit down for supper."

Jack squeezed his hand tight. The coins pressed his palm. They weren't a gift, not exactly. More like a payment of sorts, money that meant he was supposed to keep secrets.

A FAMILY MEAL

CORA CREPT DOWN the dark paneled hallway toward the light that shone from the dining room. She heard a serving dish thump on the table and the *tink* of cutlery. Late again. The second time in two days.

Uncle Robert's portrait hung opposite her, catching the dining room candlelight. A white collar skimmed his generous ears and met at a button under his chin.

"I'd better go in," she whispered to Robert. His lifeless eyes silently stared. Cora smoothed the front of her dress and entered the dining room. With no windows, the room was shrouded in shadow. Candlelight cast the table in an otherworldly glow.

Mother sat perfectly straight. "You're late. We started

without you." Her brown hair was swept back from her face in an elegant chignon. Everyone in Oakdale knew that Lauren Brindley was always the picture of grace.

"I'm sorry," Cora said. "I lost track of time."

Yesterday, after the medicine show, she'd waited as Founder's Square had emptied, then waited a few minutes more. She hadn't wanted anyone to see her go to the place where the bottles had shattered. There were dozens of pieces of slick brown glass scattered over the ground. The sharp smell of tonic still hung in the air. She'd picked up a piece without jagged edges. The glass was a token, a way to remember. Cora had taken the long way home, past the old McCall place, where she and Nettie used to explore. By then, dusk was approaching. She'd hurried, but not quickly enough.

"I assume you've remembered to wash," Mother said.

Cora nodded. She'd rinsed her hands at the pump outside.

"Have a seat." Father's wire-rimmed glasses flashed with candlelight. He cut into a thick slice of beef. "Fill your plate while the food is still warm."

Nana smiled from across the table. How tiny she looked! Her head hardly reached the top of the chair. Her white tasseled shawl was pinned in place by a brooch too heavy for her narrow shoulders.

For a few years after Grandfather died, Nana had stayed

on in their yellow house. But as her forgetfulness got worse, it was agreed she shouldn't live alone. Father and Mother had closed up the house and moved Nana upstairs. In less than two weeks, at the Auxiliary Tea, they'd celebrate her sixty-sixth birthday.

Cora reached for a bowl of potatoes.

"Where have you been?" Mother asked.

"The graveyard, mostly."

"I don't know what you do there alone. Honestly, Cora, it's a little strange."

"Leave her be, Lauren," Father said. "Our Cora likes time to herself."

"Darling. I've missed you." Nana's eyes sparkled as if she'd just noticed Cora.

"I've missed you, too." Cora hadn't spent time with Nana lately. Tomorrow she'd change that. She'd sit with Nana and ask for stories about her girlhood days. It was hard to know from day to day what Nana remembered about the present, yet fragile as her memory was, stories from her childhood came clear and strong.

"Nettie," Nana said, "it's been too long since I've seen you. Please send Cora around when you think of it. That child hasn't paid me a visit in months."

Cora's chest pinched. She looked nothing like her cousin.

Mother's fork hovered in midair. "This isn't Nettie. She's Alma's girl. This is my daughter, Cora Elizabeth."

"Oh, don't be silly," Nana said. "Nettie's always running behind. She came into this world nine days late. Don't you remember that?"

Cora leaned in so Nana could better see. "I'm Cora. The one with brown hair. We have supper together every night."

"Yes, dear." Nana smiled contentedly.

Earlier today, when she'd seen Nettie, Cora had asked what she'd thought of the show. Yesterday Nettie had squeezed Cora's arm during the exciting parts. Today Nettie shrugged. It was all right, she said, if you liked things like that. Cora took that to mean Nettie didn't.

Father set down his knife. "I heard the McCall farm sold."

"Really?" Mother said. "Who'd want that old place?"

"I don't know, but George Kennedy said he'd heard it sold in August. The new owner moved in last week."

"Someone from town?" Mother asked.

"That's not what George said."

Cora salted her boiled potatoes and mashed in butter with the back of her fork. She hadn't seen anyone there yesterday when she'd passed by after the show. No one had lived at the farm for years, not since Mr. McCall had died. The fields had been empty Cora's whole life, the farmhouse wild and overgrown. Cora and Nettie used to roam through the tangles of briars and crowded trees. That was before

Nettie had said she was too old for such childish things.

Would McCalls' feel the same now that someone had bought it? Here was another new person to meet. Cora would have to write it down in her journal. Lately, the journal Nana had given her had become a place to gather her thoughts.

"Charles," Mother said, "have you heard about a man named Kingsbury?"

Cora straightened in her chair.

"Kingsbury. The doctor, you mean? It took me half an hour to peel off the handbills he'd stuck to the front of the store."

"I heard he's selling some sort of medicine. Out on the street, no less."

"Well, yes. He runs a traveling show. Held a big one yesterday in Founder's Square."

"Nathanael had no problem with this?"

"Actually, he welcomed the man. That's what Tobias Mueller said. The show ended quickly enough. I don't expect we'll see him again."

Mother shook her head. Her earrings glinted with candlelight. "What was Nathanael thinking?"

Cora hoped Dr. Kingsbury wouldn't leave soon. She still had so many questions for Jack.

"Alma said there was quite a crowd. Who was there, I can't begin to imagine."

Cora studied her boiled potatoes, not wanting to catch her mother's eye. She'd known Mother wouldn't approve. Most of the time, Cora tried to do as she was asked. But there were so many things she wanted to know, and sometimes that got the better of her.

"It's been so dry. So very hot." Nana held out her glass. "Nettie, could you please pour me more water?"

Cora twisted her napkin in her fist. *I'm Cora,* she wanted to say, but she knew it would make no difference. Would the tonic help Nana? Would it make her mind sound?

"Almost six months with no rain," Father said. "Why would someone buy that old farm in the middle of a drought?"

Cora reached for the jug and filled Nana's glass. Nana didn't need tonic, just love and attention. Tomorrow afternoon she'd sit with her grandmother. She'd stay until there was no doubt Nana knew who she was. Come Monday, after school, she'd stop by McCalls' and take a look for herself. Maybe she'd even ask Nettie to come.

"Cora," Mother said, as though she'd only remembered, "that's two times in a row you've been late for supper. Monday you'll come home straight after school. After that, we'll see about you getting time to wander alone."

THESE SAME STARS

IT WAS DARK before they finally sat down to the fish Jack had caught for supper.

Dr. Kingsbury settled on a rock, his plate balanced on his knees. "Tell me what you learned today."

The river rushed by, as dark as the heavens. The moon gave enough light to see. "I had a hard time at first. The people here aren't too friendly."

"Hardly surprising," the doctor said. "Few people trust an outsider, not straightaway."

Jack tried to explain what he'd heard. "The mayor's family has lived here forever, the Kennedys not as long. One family makes pies and rocking chairs—the Muellers, I think?" That wasn't how the story went. Jack tried to remember what Cora had said. "I met the mayor's niece. Her name's Cora Brindley. She told me about the oak in the square. Her long-past uncle planted it. That's how the town got its name."

The doctor wiped his mouth with a handkerchief. "That explains the fence around its trunk."

"The man who started the town, Robert Frasier was his name. He wasn't the one who set up the fence. That happened later, sometime after he died. The tree helps the people of Oakdale remember how deep their roots go, Cora said. Every year, they hear the oak's story at school." The part where the oak grew so fast, that was hard for Jack to believe. "Cora says the tree took care of Frasier. Not long after planting, it grew to full size. He survived that first winter on a crop of acorns. Have you ever heard anything like it?"

"I've heard stranger things." The doctor dipped his plate in the river. With a handful of sand he scrubbed it clean. "You wouldn't guess the half of it."

"There's a celebration called Founder's Day, to remember when the tree was planted. They were hanging a banner when I was in town. It's two weeks from now."

"Founder's Day," Dr. Kingsbury said, "now that's interesting."

Jack set down his nearly empty plate and pulled off his boots and socks. The river was a comfort when he plunged his feet in, a relief from the dust and heat. He splashed his legs in the quick-moving water. The pennies in his pocket jingled. Coins he'd been paid to keep secrets.

"You've made a fine start, my boy. We'll learn more about Oakdale from our customers. We may not have many at first, but they'll come. You'll see."

"We could go back to town," Jack said. "Then everyone would know we're still here. Isaac said once that—"

The doctor stilled. "What did you say?"

"Isaac told me one time—"

Dr. Kingsbury lunged forward, overturning Jack's plate. "Do you think you know better, like that fool Isaac?" He grabbed Jack's wrist and twisted.

Don't anger the doctor, don't do it! The words raced through Jack's mind. "I'm sorry! I didn't mean—"

The pain in his arm deepened and spread.

Jack couldn't breathe. He had to stay calm.

"Forget him." Dr. Kingsbury glared. "I thought you understood, but I see I need to make myself more clear. Don't ever mention his name again."

As quick as it had happened, the doctor released him.

Jack stared at his upended plate, the last of the fish covered in dirt.

"How deep are your roots?" Dr. Kingsbury said. "That's what I want to know."

Jack's wrist throbbed. "My roots?" The words made no sense.

"How deep do they go? Are you loyal to me?"

Jack had left everything to follow the doctor. "Yes, Dr. Kingsbury. I—"

"Then don't doubt my decisions." The doctor drew close, touched the arm he'd just wrenched.

Jack tried to stay calm, but his heart wouldn't let him as it pounded in his chest.

"I know Sunday normally is your day off, but there's tonic to make and bottles to label, and without . . ." A muscle in the doctor's jaw twitched. "Without any other assistance, I need more of your time. I'll give you an hour tomorrow. That's all I will spare." Dr. Kingsbury straightened the sleeves of his coat. "We have a busy day ahead. Don't stay up too late." He took the path back to the grove, quickly swallowed in darkness.

Jack climbed the slab of stone near the river. He cradled his wrist in his lap. After the show, when the doctor had grabbed his chin, he'd known he would have to be careful. Isaac had always looked out for him. The time Jack had accidentally broken two bottles, Isaac had told the doctor he'd dropped them. When Jack had forgotten the lanterns one night, Isaac said he had left them burning.

The water raced by—steady, unending—the same river

that ran to his old fishing spot—over the hill and down the path, not very far from home. Tonight maybe Papa sat on the porch, smoking his pipe as he gazed at the stars. Maybe Ma sat next to him, rocking Lucy.

Never hold a sleeping child, Ma used to say. It makes them needy. Spoils them. But since Lucy had gotten sick, Ma ignored her own advice. She'd taken to carrying Lu most of the time, though Lu was big enough to walk. Once the illness came, she was never far from Lucy's side.

It had been awful, those weeks Lu was sick.

Jack stared at the stars. Isaac had told him some of their names. Polaris was the guiding star, that cluster of seven the Pleiades. Millions and millions brightened the sky. It made Jack feel small to consider.

As he'd caught fish for supper, he'd remembered what Mr. Ogden had said. The teacher had seen Isaac yesterday morning, possibly after the argument. Had Isaac left because of the doctor's cruelty? Maybe there had been secrets Isaac had been told to keep, too.

The doctor had mistreated his friend. For the first time, Jack wondered why Issac had stayed so long.

Their last night together, he and Isaac had studied the stars. *Pay attention,* Isaac had told him. *Don't be too quick to decide what you know.* Isaac had pointed out constellations, but there were some Jack couldn't find. He saw Scorpius's long hooked tail, but not the rest of its body. Ursa Major looked more like a cook pot than the bear Isaac described.

If things aren't clear, Isaac said, *give yourself time. You may be surprised. There's often more there than what you first see.* Before that, they'd spoken about the new town, how Dr. Kingsbury would be received.

Had Isaac only meant the stars, or had he tried to give Jack some kind of warning?

The night was still, aside from the river.

Jack picked a star out of the millions. The star was his for the night. The same one hung over his family. Right now. This very minute.

Grass crackled near the path. Jack looked, but no one was there. A squirrel or a rabbit? He couldn't tell, but something moved through the tufts of grass. He glimpsed the swish of a matted tail. A snout emerged, a hairy head.

Jack relaxed. It was only the stray. "Here, boy," he called.

For a younger dog, the mile from town would have been an easy trip. But not for this one with his years and his limp. The dog drank at the river. Once he'd had enough, he ate the abandoned scraps of fish that had fallen from the up-turned plate.

Jack pushed the fur from the dog's face. His eyes were as warm as a handful of earth.

"Bear. That's your name." It came to Jack easily. There was no better fit.

The dog nudged Jack's fingers with his wet nose.

No one in Oakdale would have bothered to name him. They treated the dog as they'd treated him—as something best to avoid.

Not Cora, though. She'd been kind.

Jack took out his carving and studied the wood. The crooked curve of the back. The odd twist of the tail. It was a cat that didn't look like a cat.

Unless that wasn't what he'd been making.

He glanced at Bear where the dog had settled. Maybe the ears looked wrong because they weren't meant to be pointed. If Jack cut a bit deeper, he could shape the harsh lines, smooth them till they flopped at the sides. The tail he could shorten. The snout he could round. He'd add the tip of a dog's panting tongue.

The wood was awakening, as Isaac had told him a true carving would. The sleek fur Jack could roughen a bit. He ran his knife across its back. "It's you. Always has been," he said to the dog who slept at his feet. "I just didn't know it yet."

If Lucy were here, she'd hang on Bear's neck and laugh as he licked her cheeks. She'd love this wooden dog she could hold in her hands. Jack tried to picture Lu's face, the dimple that flashed when she smiled. So much could change in a year. When would they head back to Covington? An eighteen-month trip, the doctor had said.

Lu might not know him when he got home. He promised himself when he got there, he'd appreciate the everyday moments with her—a piggyback ride, a walk to the river. Those were the things he thought of most now.

He had at least four months more with the doctor without Isaac's protection.

Jack shoved the carving deep in his pocket. A twinge of pain shot through his wrist.

How would he make it without Isaac's guidance? Without someone to keep him from harm?

RUMORS AND TALES

SILAS MET EVANGELINE in the cool of the morning. They'd talk of everything:

When would the goldfinches brood in their nests?

Was there ever a scent sweeter than lilacs?

What made the crickets sing?

Sometimes he'd find her in the evening light, when the moon settled over the trees. Evangeline had an inquisitive mind and a laugh as light as the stars. She was one year younger than Silas, as eager as he was for a friend.

One question Evangeline asked him most often: Do you think it will rain again soon?

"Of course it will rain," Silas said, but the question

made him uncomfortable. It was too much like the talk he'd heard from the boys.

In the last month, the heat had intensified. Thunderclouds formed without spilling rain. It was strange, Henry said, how the drought had arrived not long after Silas. As they tried to salvage the last of the wheat, the boys spun their wild tales:

Silas was the reason the wheat had withered.

His coming had lowered the river water and dried up the wells in town.

Because of Silas, Oakdale was left with very little to eat.

It was foolishness. All of it.

Still the drought that had driven him from his home made its home in Oakdale now. He couldn't explain why it had happened, if it was coincidence or something more.

"Things would be different," Henry said, "if my brother had gotten your job."

Silas had to hang on. He had no other choice but to do his work. When it was clear the harvest was almost done—most of it useless on account of the heat—he asked Mr. McCall if afterward he could help with work in the barn. He needed the job and its steady pay, even though he didn't make much.

He also wasn't yet ready to leave Evangeline.

A WOODEN RABBIT

SUNDAY AFTERNOON, JACK plunged his cup into the river's current. His hand ached as cold water slid over his skin. This was his first drink since daybreak, the only moment he'd had to himself. He pressed the cup to the back of his neck before its chill faded away.

He had an hour, the doctor had told him, before he was needed again. It was just enough time to cool off in the river. Jack stripped down and waded in. Where the river deepened, he shoved off the bottom and floated on his back. The water enveloped his body as he stared at the empty sky.

The day he'd first seen Dr. Kingsbury, the sky was the same cloudless expanse. His neighbor, Mrs. Anderson, had come to the house with news of the doctor. Jack had left with the promise to come back with tonic. He'd walked through town that afternoon, the streets deserted and shops closed. A crowd milled around a mysterious wagon, its wood burnished and gleaming.

"Come," a voice called, and the crowd drew closer. "Come if you're tired or sickly or weak."

Dr. Kingsbury was as graceful as the cranes that swooped in the fields during planting season. His eyes were deep set, his limbs long and thin. Hair as dark as his eyes skimmed his shoulders. A poppy adorned his buttonhole. Though the road was dusty, not a speck of dirt marred the legs of the trousers he wore.

The doctor studied the crowd before him. "There are some here who ache for relief, who long for their health to be restored." He stopped speaking when his eyes met Jack's. A few turned to see who had caught his attention. "There are some who have come as their very last hope."

Jack hardly dared move, his whole body rooted.

"How bad is the sickness?" Dr. Kingsbury asked when later Jack reached the front of the line.

"It's gone on for weeks."

"Your brother? A sister, perhaps?"

"My sister. How did you know?"

"I see that you carry a burden, though you yourself look healthy and strong."

"I don't have any money, but I need some tonic. My sister has to get better."

The doctor pressed a bottle into Jack's hand. "Give your sister a dose as soon as you can. Follow up with another tomorrow. If she won't swallow it, pour some on a rag and use it to dampen her skin."

"How can I pay you for this?"

"I could use a boy," Dr. Kingsbury said. "Come back tomorrow with news of your sister. You can help with my show while I'm here in town."

"What if it doesn't . . . ?" Jack couldn't finish. What if the tonic wasn't enough?

The doctor surrounded Jack's hands with his own. "This will help. You have to believe."

He'd believed. With his whole heart he'd trusted.

Jack shut his eyes. The river thrummed in his ears. Water soothed his swollen wrist as it lapped against his side.

The next morning, he'd gone back to the doctor with news of Lucy. Her fever had broken. She'd asked for a piece of bread. All day, as he'd helped Dr. Kingsbury work, he'd let his heart hope that Lu would get stronger. When Papa came in the evening, he shook the doctor's hand. "She's almost herself again. We can't thank you enough for what you've done. How can we ever repay you?"

"Let your son come with me. I'll give him a job," Dr. Kingsbury said. "He'll mail his wages home every month.

I'll be back this way in a year and a half. After that, he can go, or he can stay on."

Jack's parents discussed it at supper that night. By morning, they'd agreed. They were indebted to the man. If the doctor wanted Jack as an assistant, he could go with their blessing. It was the least they could do, offering his service, after the doctor had healed Lucy.

Jack swam until his feet touched the river bottom. His gaze drifted over the bank. The willow trees had disappeared. The rock where he'd watched the stars was gone. The current must have carried him farther downriver than he'd ever been. Jack hid in the reeds along the bank. What time was it? He had to hurry.

He could swim to the grove, fighting the current, or run, naked, though the underbrush. Jack was a good swimmer, but he tired easily. Running was quicker. Hopefully, no one would see.

He dove into the bushes at the river's edge. Branches scraped his legs as he ran; pebbles poked his feet. The fire of nettles prickled his skin. He pushed through a thicket of hazelnut saplings. There was something soft under his heel. Jack bent down to see what it was. Shoved back in the shadows was a knapsack, a piece of string twisted around one strap.

The bag was Isaac's. He must be nearby. Had he been so close all along?

"Isaac!" Jack shouted. "Are you there?"

But Jack only heard the rush of the river.

Maybe Isaac was fishing farther downstream.

Jack could borrow Isaac's clothes and later come back to return them. He opened the bag and pulled out a shirt. A small wooden rabbit tumbled to the ground. Isaac's carving, the one he had worked on their last night together. Jack cupped the creature in his hand. The rabbit crouched, its body ready to spring. Isaac had breathed life into it. Jack hoped one day he'd learn Isaac's secret. He pulled on the shirt, tucked the rabbit away, and pushed the bag deep in the thicket.

It didn't take long for Jack to reach the spot where he'd left his clothes. Once dressed, he shook out Isaac's shirt, hoping to rid it of a few clinging leaves. A rolled-up piece of paper fell from the pocket, a piece no bigger than a beetle. Carefully, Jack unwound the strip. The writing was in Isaac's hand:

Ernest McPherson.

It wasn't a name he'd heard before.

He slipped the paper into his pocket, then stashed Isaac's shirt behind the reeds. Good. There was no way to see where he'd hidden it.

"I gave you an hour."

Jack whipped around.

"One hour," Dr. Kingsbury said, "not the two you've taken."

"I was lost. A current took me downriver. I've just gotten back," Jack said.

The doctor's eyes narrowed. "Since you've freely taken an hour of my time, I'll take an hour of yours. There'll be no supper for you tonight. You'll scrub the dirt off the wagon instead. If I decide that you've gotten it clean enough, you can eat again in the morning."

Jack's shoulders slumped. He was tired and hungry. How long had the doctor been standing there? What exactly had he seen?

A HEADACHE APPEASED

IT HAD A bite, Miss Moore couldn't deny. The tonic burned as she swallowed a spoonful. There was a wisp of a flavor she couldn't place, at once both strong and soothing. She hadn't planned on taking the medicine. The only reason she'd bought a bottle was as an excuse to see Elijah Kingsbury.

That was before her vision had shimmered. Before she'd shut her eyes and seen flashes of light. A headache was coming, she knew the signs, and the last one had only stopped yesterday. What a way to start a Monday morning!

She pushed the cork back in the bottle and set it next to a letter from home.

She'd seen him. Up close. Still she couldn't place him.

Earlier, before opening the shop, Miss Moore had gone to the grove. She hadn't been the only one. Half a dozen others had beaten her there, waiting in the unbearable heat. She'd fanned herself with her bonnet and joined the back of the line.

Ahead of her was Mrs. Kennedy, her brown fingers swollen and bent. "It's been an age since I've sewn without pain," she said to the Reverend, who stood next in line.

Reverend Wells mopped his face with a handkerchief. "I'm sorry to hear your rheumatism's bothering you, Mrs. Kennedy."

The closer the line drew to the wagon, the better Miss Moore could see. The cupboard door was again filled with bottles. Mrs. Mueller stood at the front of the line. She held her youngest, a wailing redhead who swung his tiny fists. Dr. Kingsbury gave her a bottle of tonic. She dipped in her finger as the doctor had demonstrated and rubbed her baby's gums. The little boy blinked. His hands grew still.

Mrs. Kennedy touched the Reverend's sleeve. "What are you here for, if you don't mind my asking?"

"To see the doctor up close, I suppose. Martha came home filled with stories. My Annie hasn't let go of the poppy he gave her, though it's lost most of its petals. Honestly, I'm not sure what to think. This man says he can cure every ailment, but God's the Great Healer, not some bottle of tonic."

"Now, Reverend," Mrs. Kennedy said, "sometimes God uses everyday people to do His work. You should know that."

"How might I help you?" the doctor asked when Miss Moore reached the front of the line. His diction was as smooth as a finely tuned cello.

"I'm here . . ." For an instant, Miss Moore lost her bearings. "I'm here for a bottle of tonic."

There was an unwavering set to his eyes. "Yes, of course. May I ask after your trouble?"

Her trouble was she couldn't remember where she'd seen him before, though she'd racked her mind trying. "I'm not . . ." She stopped. "I don't think . . . I'd rather not say, if you understand."

"My apologies, Mrs. . . . ?"

Eloise stiffened. "My name is *Miss* Moore."

"Miss Moore. I see." Dr. Kingsbury lowered his voice. "If your concern involves finding a husband . . ."

For heaven's sake! Why was it people always assumed she was in need of company? "My *concern*," she said, "is mine alone." Miss Moore pulled the coins from her purse and dropped them in the doctor's palm.

His fingers closed over the money, fingers she knew she'd seen before.

As he sent the boy to fetch a bottle, Miss Moore studied the doctor. His nose was sharp, his jawline severe. That dark hair, a stark contrast to his pale complexion.

Where was it she'd seen him? In a shop? On the street?

Could it have been at the concert in City Park, where her parents had taken her as a child? The orchestra had played such beautiful music, Miss Moore had imagined winging away, like a kite above the trees.

"Do you only travel the roads of Ohio or have you been to other states, too?"

"That's an interesting question," Dr. Kingsbury said. "Why do you ask?"

"You seem familiar, that's all, like someone I've met."

He laughed. "I can't imagine many share my resemblance."

She smiled. That was certainly true.

As she'd waited in line, she'd heard him claim his tonic could do a number of things. He'd told Mrs. Kennedy it relieved stiff joints. Soak your hands in a bowl of tonic and water, and the pain practically disappeared. He'd encouraged the Reverend to try the tonic to help him focus while writing his sermons.

Dr. Kingsbury was like a fortune-teller who spun beguiling stories, a performer who changed those stories to suit his listener's needs.

"Indiana," she said. "Ever been there?"

He tapped his lip, thinking. "If I have, it was years ago. There have been so many places, I don't always remember where I've stopped."

"Here you go," said the boy. Gray eyes peeked from beneath his ragged hair as he handed her the bottle. *Where'd you meet the doctor?* she wanted to ask. *What are you doing with him?* But she knew no child who needed to work must have much say in the matter.

She'd gained nothing from her time in the grove, except for the bottle of tonic.

The wavering lines in her vision had faded; a headache would follow soon. Miss Moore rubbed her temples, where the pain always started, but this time nothing was there. No ache pulsed through her forehead or squeezed her neck.

Had it really worked, Dr. Kingsbury's tonic?

The headache she'd dreaded since leaving the grove had ended before it began.

LIKE A DRAGONFLY'S WING

THE AFTERNOON WAS heavy with heat. A scattering of clouds dotted the sky. Mr. Ogden welcomed the sounds of chatter as his students explored the riverbed. It had been months since their last nature hike, two days since he'd started the tonic.

So far, since beginning the medicine, Walter Ogden had only seen little changes. Yesterday the tremors hadn't come until he was already at church. It had made him so hopeful, that handful of hours when he'd felt like himself again. But that hope had vanished when the symptoms returned.

His hand shook at the most inconvenient of times. His foot was troublesome, seizing up as he walked. How long would he have to live like this?

"Cuthbert, stop!" Nettie screeched. "Keep that bug away from me!"

The boy buzzed his lips, an arm outstretched, as he chased after his sister.

"Cuthbert! Enough. Leave Nettie alone."

Cuthbert stopped, his pomade-slick hair flopping over his forehead, and peered into his palm. Nettie ran beyond the trees, till there was plenty of distance between them.

"What's that you've got?" Mr. Ogden said.

The boy smiled. "A dragonfly." His crooked teeth were too big for his face. "We could add it to our bug collection."

Cuthbert James was a challenge at times, but his curiosity was equally strong.

"Wonderful. Let me come see."

The students were busy collecting their specimens. Janie Kennedy flitted past like a finch, feathers gripped in her golden-brown fingers. Thomas Mueller sat hunched on the ground, poking a stick to unearth a stone. Nettie joined Cora down at the river to sort through a pile of leaves.

Cuthbert lifted his palm. "It's a blue darner, I think."

Blue and black patterned the thin abdomen, its beautiful wings, light and translucent, like tiny panes of glass. "May I see it up close?"

Cuthbert nodded, a hank of hair standing on end.

It was a wonder Cuthbert had found a blue darner still in one piece. Dragonflies' fragile bodies broke easily.

Without thinking, Mr. Ogden reached out. As he touched the insect, his fingers quaked. Quickly he snatched back his hand.

"It's all right, Mr. Ogden. The dragonfly's dead. It can't hurt you now."

Cuthbert hadn't seen his fingers shake. Mr. Ogden tried to laugh to hide his embarrassment. "No, of course it won't. What was I thinking?" He reached for the insect again, this time with his other hand.

Since Saturday, hope, fragile and buoyant as a dragonfly's wing, had never been far from his thoughts. It had only been a couple of days, but with so little change in his symptoms, he was finding it hard to hold on.

"How's that toe of yours, Cuthbert?" Benjamin asked as he came from the river. The front of his trousers was streaked with mud, his cheeks red with heat.

"The nail's purpled. It almost fell off. Nettie's taking me to buy tonic today. That'll fix it up quick."

Somewhere nearby Mr. Ogden heard voices, not from the children but farther on. It sounded as though they came from the road.

People probably going to see the doctor. Interest in the man was growing. The willow grove wasn't far from here. On Saturday, as he'd left the doctor, Mr. Ogden hadn't passed anyone. Yesterday at church, there'd been plenty of talk, mainly stories about George Kennedy's healing. By this morning, on his way to school, Mr. Ogden had seen a number of people walking to the grove.

Dr. Kingsbury didn't have a traditional practice. While he'd probably never trained in a hospital, he'd known of the palsy immediately. The doctor was a self-taught man who'd done his learning on the road.

Benjamin held up a grimy hand. "I've already got a pile of specimens. Rocks and bark. All sorts of things. Can I go see who's there?"

"I'm afraid not," Mr. Ogden said. "If you're done collecting, you could help Cuthbert find a leaf to carry his dragonfly."

"Oh, all right," the boy said, shoving his things in his pockets. "Cuthbert, come on."

"Mr. Ogden!" A halo of curls surrounded Janie's worried face. She kicked up dust as she ran to him. "I've lost one of my wings!"

They searched the places she'd been, trying to find the missing feather, but couldn't see it anywhere. "You can have the one I keep on my desk. Help yourself when we get back to school."

"Thank you," she said, hugging him before she flew off again.

Cuthbert and Benjamin returned, bundles of elm leaves in their hands. Their faces were smudged with dirt and sweat. The students had been out long enough. It was close to the end of the school day. "Come, everyone, gather your specimens. Cora, could you help with the younger students?"

But there was no answer.

Mr. Ogden went to the spot near the river where he'd last seen Cora and Nettie. All he found was a pile of leaves. "Cora. Nettie," he called. "It's time to go." He walked farther along the riverbed and called for them again.

The others hadn't seen the girls. The last anyone could remember was the two of them, down at the river.

Fear gripped Mr. Ogden. The girls were sensible enough to stay out of the water, but what if they'd come to some other harm?

He'd spent so much time wrapped in his thoughts, he'd forgotten the most important thing—his students and their well-being.

"Come," he shouted. "Everyone. Each older child pair with a younger one. Follow behind. Stay out of the river." He led them along the riverbed. From the bank, he could see the doctor's wagon and a patch of blue racing across the green meadow. It was Nettie running to him.

"Mr. Ogden, I'm sorry. We were looking for leaves, and—"

"Where's Cora gone?"

Nettie stared at the ground. She pointed to the willow grove.

"Wait here," he told everyone, and hurried on as best he could through the brambles and branches and into the grove. He found the girl behind a curtain of willows, watching the people who waited nearby.

"Cora Brindley." He tried to hold his voice steady, to let go of the anger and fear welling in him. She was all right, safe and sound.

Cora started when she heard her name.

"What were you thinking, coming here without my permission?"

She rippled the branches with her fingers, refusing to look at him. "The willows have such interesting leaves. I thought Nettie and I could pick some and add them to our collection."

"You can't just leave the rest of the class. Do you understand?"

She met his gaze, her brown eyes solemn, and slowly nodded her head.

"I'll have to talk to your parents about this."

"No, please, Mr. Ogden. Don't do that!"

"That's not for you to decide. Now, come." He guided Cora by the elbow, determined not to lose her again. Once they reached the others, he said, "We must get to school. Nettie. Please lead us back to the road."

Nettie pinched her lips together, her freckled cheeks pale as she glanced at Cora, and took her place at the front of the line. Thomas, his pockets stuffed with rocks, followed Benjamin and Cuthbert, who carried the dragonfly between them on a stretcher of leaves. Then came Samantha and Janie Kennedy, the Thompson twins, and the Griffins.

He waited until everyone had passed and fell in with Cora, who was last in line. She clasped her hands behind her back, watching her shoes as she walked. The leaves she and Nettie had collected had been left in a pile at the riverbed.

Of course, it wasn't leaves Cora had been after, but what was happening in the grove. He understood the fascination.

"Besides the willows, what else did you see?"

Cora spoke of the wagon and the long snaking line that twisted through the trees. More and more people were drawn to the doctor—his miracle cure, the mystery.

McCALLS' FARM

CORA LIMPED AS she neared McCalls' farm, her knee scraped and bloodied. She'd tripped as she'd run from the grove after school, after Nettie had seen her and threatened to tell. She'd tried to keep running as long as she could, far from the grove and the road back to town, until she saw the old wooden fence that bordered the edge of McCalls'. When she reached it, she rested her head on a post. Brambles twisted through the railing beneath her. In the overgrown fields grasshoppers whirred in the asters and goldenrod.

Mother had said she had to come home after school; she'd done as Mother had asked. But not long after, she'd slipped out again. Not just to be stubborn—she wasn't like that—but sometimes she couldn't help herself. There was so much she wanted to know! She wanted to see the doctor at work and talk with Jack again.

And she had talked to Jack for a couple of minutes. She'd shown him the broken piece of glass. The tonic smelled both familiar and strange. How? She wanted to learn. She'd even heard whispers from those waiting in line that maybe the tonic could bring back the rain.

As she started to leave, she'd seen Nettie and Cuthbert, at the back of the line in the shade of the trees.

Nettie held her arms rigid. Her lips had gone white. "What are you doing here?"

"What do you mean? I told you earlier I wanted to come, especially since our time was cut short during the nature walk."

"Why were you talking to him? That boy?"

"Him?" Cora said. "You mean Jack?"

Cuthbert craned to see what was happening farther ahead in the line.

Nettie set her hands firm on her hips. "Oh, Jack's his name, is it? So you're friends with him now?"

Why was Nettie so upset? "I don't understand what—"

Nettie pinched her lips in a scowl. "And *I* don't understand what's come over you. You weren't like this before."

She grabbed her brother's hand, yanking him out of line. "Come on, Cuth, let's go. We'll try again later, when it isn't so busy."

Cuthbert groaned. "Can't we wait? It won't be so bad. The line will start moving any minute."

But Nettie wouldn't listen to him. She pulled Cuthbert down the shaded path, turning before they got very far. "I'm sure Aunt Lauren will want to know the two of us saw you here."

Cora kicked her toe against the fence railing. It wasn't fair Nettie got to take Cuthbert. She hadn't even wanted to go. If Aunt Alma had asked Cora instead, she would have helped, straightaway. But Aunt Alma hadn't, and anyhow, Cora didn't have Mother's permission.

What if today had been it, her last chance to see Jack?

She lifted her head and let her eyes wander. The farmhouse was set back in the field. Once white, the old house had weathered and grayed. The front steps were missing, the porch had caved in, but it must have been beautiful long ago. Behind were the woods she and Nettie had loved, where they'd stained their fingers with blackberries and laughed and played and dreamed. But that had been a while ago. Whoever had bought the old place, Cora hoped they wouldn't clear all the briars or cut down the overgrown trees.

"You all right over there?"

In the field was the man with the silvery beard, the one

she'd seen at the medicine show. He worked near a wagon loaded with wood. Was he the one who'd bought McCalls'?

She raised her voice loud enough he could hear. "I fell. My knee's pretty bad."

The man met Cora at the fence. "Here," he said. "Take my handkerchief." A breeze stirred the cloth as he handed it to her.

She wiped up the blood as best she could.

The man offered his hand. "I'm Silas Carey, but you can call me Silas."

She'd never used a grown-up's first name. "I'm Cora."

He waved his hand when she held out the hankie. "Go ahead. You can keep it."

"Are you the one who bought this place?"

"I am," Silas said. "This spot was too pretty for me to pass up. 'Course it will be prettier once it rains."

Cora thought of what she'd heard in the grove. "Some say the tonic can bring back the rain."

Silas turned his head. "Do they now?"

"Just wait till you see this field filled with flowers." The asters and goldenrod were only a taste of the farm's wild beauty. "Where'd you come from?" Cora asked.

"No one place in particular. Lived all over, I guess you could say."

"How'd you hear about Oakdale?"

Silas looked over the field. His eyes were a color she

couldn't quite catch. "I worked here one summer when I was a boy. Speaking of work, if you don't mind me asking, I could use a hand with those boards in my wagon. That is, if you're feeling all right."

Her knee looked better. The scrape wasn't so bad. She slipped through the fence and followed him. "Are you planning on building something?"

"I'm going to put up a barn."

Cora had never seen a barn here before, but she noticed the field had already been leveled. A barn would be a lot of work for one man on his own.

Silas pulled a board from the wagon bed. Cora grabbed the other end. "How'd you bang up that knee?" he asked.

"I fell leaving the grove."

"Visiting that Dr. Kingsbury?" They set the board down and returned to the wagon. "That's where you heard about his tonic bringing rain?"

"Well, yes. I mean, no, not exactly. I'd gone to visit Jack. He's the boy who works for the doctor."

Silas grabbed another board. "A friend of yours?"

He was, Cora realized, as she lifted her end, the wood rough in her hands.

They worked on together, until they'd emptied the wagon. "You're good at this, you know that?" Silas said. "Ever thought of building a barn?"

Of course she hadn't, but she couldn't help smiling. "I better go," she said.

"Thanks for your help. Stop by anytime."

Cora waved goodbye as she climbed through the fence.

There were rules in this town. Rules about strangers. *Don't be too familiar. Let them pass on. If strangers stay, don't be quick to befriend them.*

She'd broken those rules twice over now.

A BURNING

ONE QUIET NIGHT, the fire started.

Only when the horses screamed did Silas know something was wrong. An orange glow lit the barn's back wall. Smoke gathered beneath the high-pitched roof.

In the hayloft, Silas pushed off his blanket. There was no time to question or think. He covered his face and crawled to the ladder, the heat so close he could hardly breathe. Down he climbed through the flames to make his escape.

The horses shrieked and tossed their heads. Silas raced to the stalls. "Get on!" he shouted as he set them loose. They escaped before the wall folded in.

Before he could reach the farmhouse to warn them, the

McCalls ran from inside. "Get to town!" the mister roared. "Ring the church bell! Tell everyone to bring buckets."

At least a dozen men rushed to the farm, ready to put out the fire. Into the night, the fire burned. It raged beyond the fields and consumed the north part of town. The church, the schoolhouse, and a couple of homes, all were lost to the fire. The flames had poured across the square but stopped before they reached the oak. In the morning, all that was left of the barn was a smoldering pile of coals.

Silas's eyes had burned for days. His lungs were seared, his throat raw from the smoke.

He'd saved every one of the horses, but McCall never thanked him for it. Instead the man blamed him for the fire. No matter it started on the side of the barn far from the hayloft where Silas slept. Townsfolk whispered Silas kept a lantern up there. That the fire had started when he knocked it over. Others said he might have been smoking, when he'd never even tried tobacco before.

Those rumors were the kinder ones.

The lowest story, the one that caught on, was the one Henry whispered to Bill and Ray. The one where Silas set the fire on purpose.

That story spread all over town. It had power the truth didn't hold.

McCall didn't care how hard Silas had worked, that he'd stayed in the fields long after the others and done extra work in the barn. McCall's trust disappeared and with it his kindness. "Hand over your wages," he said. "That's the first of what you owe from the fire. You'll sleep in the fields till you've worked off the rest, a couple of weeks, maybe more."

Silas wasn't sure what had started the fire. The rainless weeks had baked the earth dry and parched every board in the barn. Henry and his friends were as hard and brittle. Silas said he'd been sleeping when the fire had caught, but they told him that couldn't be true. They'd decided already that he was a boy who lived on close terms with trouble.

Evangeline. Had she accepted that story? Had she believed he'd burned the barn down? He never knew. After the fire, he'd avoided her. He'd never seen her again.

When three weeks were done, McCall called him over. He handed Silas a meal from the missus and told him he had to go. "Do you know what you said when I hired you on? 'I promise, Mr. McCall. I won't disappoint you.' You remember that?"

Miserably, Silas nodded.

Mr. McCall spat on the ground. "Too bad that wasn't true."

PROMISES MADE

THE LAST OF the sunset burned the horizon, casting the grove in shadow. Jack rested on the wagon's porch, Bear asleep beside him. The dog had stayed close since Saturday night, following him everywhere.

"Dr. Kingsbury? Could I have a moment?"

Jack strained to see who called from the path.

Dr. Kingsbury rose. "Yes, certainly." His white sleeves disappeared in the gloom of his coat.

Maybe the man wanted some tonic. They'd spent most of yesterday preparing a batch. A number of customers had come today, just as the doctor predicted. At times, there had been a few dozen at once. Even Cora had come to talk to him.

The doctor cut across the grove. This was Jack's chance to study Isaac's note. He nudged Bear aside and took it from his pocket. Unrolling the strip, he tilted it to catch the last of the sun. *Ernest McPherson.* The name was written in faded blue ink. Two lines underscored the letter *c.* There were no other marks, no indication of who Ernest McPherson might be.

Last night, Jack had quickly scrubbed down the wagon. He'd left the bucket and brush by the riverbed and fetched Isaac's shirt from its hiding place. The sun had sunk below the horizon by the time he'd reached the thicket. He'd hoped to find Isaac, back from fishing, or wherever he'd been in the hours before, but no one was there. Isaac's bag lay where Jack had left it, still rumpled from his hasty retreat. Silence shrouded the trees, a hush only broken by the buzz of cicadas.

Jack rolled up the paper again. All day as he'd worked, he'd thought about Isaac. Where had he gone? Had he fallen somewhere and broken his leg? Had a wild animal injured him?

Until after, Isaac had said on Friday morning when they'd come to town. He'd given Jack their salute. When they'd said goodbye to each other, Jack was sure Isaac had no plans of leaving.

"Jack?" the doctor called.

Two figures emerged from the shadowed grove. Dr. Kingsbury took down a lantern to light. Jack shielded his eyes from the flame.

"There you are," the doctor said. "Mayor James told me an incredible story, one I want you to hear."

The mayor wore a nightshirt tucked into his trousers. A shadow of whiskers covered his cheeks. "We've had a miracle brought on by the tonic! I came to the grove as soon as I heard."

A chill prickled Jack's skin. It never took long for a miracle. They happened in every town.

"Henry Graham has always used a crutch." Mayor James shook his head. "No, let me start again. Before today, Henry used a crutch. Now he's walking on his own!"

"The mayor has asked for a second show. Saturday at three o'clock."

"Please, Jack," the mayor said, "tell your story. I've asked Henry the same, and he's agreed."

Jack didn't know how to answer him.

"Not everyone here supports the doctor. Your story could change that. For the good of my town and those living nearby. Tell them about the tonic."

Jack thought of the heat and the wobbly stool. This time neither could be an excuse. He thought of the memory in the wagon—of Isaac confronting the doctor.

Whatever had happened, Jack would find out. He owed that much to his friend.

Dr. Kingsbury gripped Jack's shoulder, hard enough it burned. "You won't be disappointed in this boy. I can promise you that."

TOO MUCH TO BELIEVE

BOLTS OF FABRIC in all colors and hues lined the shelves of the general store. Items filled every available space. Silas saw lanterns tucked behind the back counter. Nails of all sizes filled small wooden boxes. A tattered calendar hung from a peg on the wall.

The counter, a worn slab of dark wood, held jars of gumdrops and licorice ropes. As a boy, Silas had studied those jars when he'd brought eggs to sell for Mrs. McCall. He'd dreamed of the taste of a gumdrop or two, but he'd never once cheated, spending her pennies. He'd taken each one of them back to the missus.

Silas breathed the familiar musty smell. In fifty-one years, the store hadn't changed.

"May I help you?" a man in an apron said.

Silas studied the man's bespectacled face, the tufted brows resting over the frames. His wiry build—Silas couldn't quite place him. "Are you Brindley?"

"I am."

This Brindley was too young for Silas to know. "Must be your father I'm remembering. It's been an age since I've been in this store." That summer Silas had first come to town, the store had been Brindley's then, too.

"Must be," the man said. "My grandfather opened the place years ago. We've been Brindley-run ever since. You'll let me know if you need anything?"

"Thank you. I will."

Silas hadn't brought much when he'd come to town over a week ago. It was food he needed. Some sustenance. He picked a few apples from a display, a mountain of greens and golds.

He'd been gone a long time. Long enough for some in Oakdale to die, for some to leave, for some to forget. Silas had never been welcomed here, but as far as he'd wandered, his thoughts circled back—to this town, the fire, Evangeline.

The bell rang at the front of the store as Dr. Kingsbury pushed the door open. The air seemed to shift as he approached, an unsettling stir that followed him.

"Afternoon," Silas said.

The doctor nodded.

A man who kept his thoughts to himself learned a number of interesting things. Silas had been to the sawmill three times for boards, where gossip centered around the doctor. How the doctor had cured Mr. Kennedy. How Kennedy's wife had bought tonic, too. How every day more folks went to the man who'd set himself up in the grove.

Silas examined a misshapen apple. On one side its skin was crisp and firm, but the other had softened and browned. Then there was that story Cora had told him yesterday afternoon, a rumor the tonic could bring on the rain. After she'd left, he'd gone to the grove, intent on hearing more. Put a bottle near a window, the story went. Let the air drink it in. Once the skies had swallowed enough, the heavens would rupture with storms.

Maybe the doctor could heal a man's ailments, but this was too much to believe.

"Can you tell me where Mr. Brindley is?" Dr. Kingsbury said.

"I think he's gone to the back of the store."

What an odd man the doctor was, wearing a coat that brushed his knees, as though the heat meant nothing to him. And those eyes, as vivid as fire-plucked coals. There was something behind them Silas couldn't name.

That summer, years ago, would the people of Oakdale have flocked to the doctor? Would they have trusted a tonic to fix the drought? Silas couldn't say why one man scoffed and another one believed.

The day McCall had let him go, Silas had left in search of more work. He'd found a couple of jobs but never made much money. His family had struggled. They'd lost their farm and had to move into Covington. It was Silas's wages that kept them afloat. What started as a few months away stretched to years before Silas finally went home.

He picked one last apple from the display. He could do with some cans of peaches and plums. There was flour he needed, bacon, too. Mr. Brindley would have to help him find those. Silas walked to the back of the store.

A bolt of cloth lay on the counter where Mr. Brindley had unfolded it. He lifted his scissors and snipped a line straight down its middle.

Dr. Kingsbury waited until he was done. "You do business in Greenville, I suspect."

"I do," Mr. Brindley said.

"Good to hear. I've got things I need to order. More bottles, some notices to print." The doctor held out a paper to him. "Everything's written down."

Mr. Brindley set his scissors aside and adjusted his glasses to read. "You're planning a show for Saturday? That's in four days. I'm not sure how quickly you'll get these things."

During his travels, Silas had heard a story in a parish

not far from New Orleans. A tale about a swamp creature whose name twisted his tongue. Dark and dangerous the beast was, with a name as strange as a wolf's lonely cry.

The doctor's gaze swept the store, lingering on Silas. "Could we continue this conversation in private?"

"Certainly." Mr. Brindley opened a door behind the counter. "Follow me."

Loup Garou. That was the swamp creature's name. Half beast, half man, it was said. Feral. Fierce. Covered in hair. The Loup Garou roamed in the dead of night.

Dr. Kingsbury wasn't a beast, not that Silas could see. Still, something about him wasn't quite right. Like that misshapen apple he'd put back with the others. The one, he suspected, that had rotted straight to its core.

What about the boy? Cora's friend. How was he faring, working for a man like him?

The office door opened. "I'll do my best to have your order ready tomorrow," Mr. Brindley was saying. The doctor thanked him, said he'd be back soon. The air stirred as he brushed past. Silas watched the bells jingle as he opened the door. The doctor stepped out to the clouds rolling in, to the dust and the sun and the gentle breeze.

Silas had come to town with a purpose; it seemed the doctor had come with his own.

"Excuse me, sir? Do you need any help?"

Silas told Mr. Brindley his order. He watched as the

man measured out flour and wrapped bacon in a square of brown paper. "Two new men in town in less than a week," Mr. Brindley said. "That doesn't happen here much. Are you the one who bought Joe McCall's place?"

Silas nodded. Since that summer, he'd mostly kept to the road with no permanent home. That summer had changed him. For the good, for the bad—he wasn't sure anymore.

Every so often, he'd pass though Oakdale because of a promise he'd made. He'd watched as the town fenced off the oak. He'd seen the fields flourish after the drought. On every visit, he'd passed by McCalls', looking for Evangeline. He'd watched the place return to the woods, wild and overgrown. Six years ago he'd heard McCall died. He'd been saving his money ever since.

"George Kennedy said the man who moved in had almost bought all his boards."

"I'm putting the barn up again." Saying it emboldened him.

Mr. Brindley rang up the order. "Well, now, how about that."

How about it, Silas thought to himself. He wasn't done with Oakdale quite yet. He belonged here, sure as anyone did.

INSIDE THE WAGON

JACK PROPPED THE door open with the wobbly stool and touched a match to the candlewicks. The wooden walls shimmered with light. In his year with the doctor, he'd been in the wagon just a handful of times. He wasn't supposed to come in on his own.

Why had he never questioned it?

The doctor had gone to town on an errand. He hadn't said when he'd be back. Yesterday, Cora had come to the grove, asking about the tonic. Jack had been thinking about it, too. What was in it besides snakeroot and ginger? Why didn't it work the same for everyone? How exactly had it cured Lucy? Had it helped her sleep and that lowered her fever? Or had it awoken her hunger and some nourishment

had helped her body to heal? If there were answers, they
had to be in the wagon.

Jack glanced outside, looking for Bear, who'd tried to
follow him in. The dog had settled himself under a willow
tree. For such a small space, the wagon was full. Jack wasn't
sure how to begin.

Papers and jars cluttered the desk. Candles stuck to the
wood in pools of wax. Alongside a spoon sat a half-empty
bottle with a poppy tucked inside. He unscrewed a few lids
from the jars. The wagon filled with the pungent scents of
alfalfa and ginger and rosemary. He picked up a journal
from the back of the desk. The doctor had written in it
yesterday:

Monday, October 10, 1887

*Oakdale, Ohio. 617 citizens. A town fairly well off with
a schoolhouse, a church, a bank, a millinery. Mayor
Nathanael James is supportive, though at first he was
not. Restored George Kennedy's hearing. Sales started
slowly but are improving. We had about sixty stop by
today. All here long for rain. Robert Frasier planted
the oak in the square. Founder's Day will be celebrated
October 22.*

October 22. Eleven days from now.

Jack turned to the beginning. *August 13, 1881. Bought*

the wagon from Kilmer, the first entry read. Dr. Kingsbury had made meticulous entries about each town where he'd stopped. There were records of healings. Reports on sales. The number of days he'd stayed in each place. The doctor had traveled through Pennsylvania, Indiana, Missouri, and Illinois. Even Isaac was mentioned—four years ago, on the day he'd joined the medicine show. Jack flipped to the page where he'd started reading and set the journal aside.

Behind the desk was a bookcase. Jack traced his fingers over the spines. *The Code of Health and Longevity. A Manual of Medical Diagnosis. Household Medicine and Surgery. Culpeper's Complete Herbal. Dr. Kilmer's Swamp Root Kidney, Liver, and Bladder Cure.*

Kilmer. That was the man who'd sold the wagon. Jack took the book down from the shelf. It was light in his hand, the pages soft from turning. Some parts of the book had been underlined. Inside was a drawing of a medicine bottle not unlike Dr. Kingsbury's. Jack read the portion beneath it:

Dr. Kilmer's Swamp Root Kidney, Liver, and Bladder Cure works wonders! Better than vegetable bitters, superior to bloodletting, surpassing all other medicines. Swamp Root heals <u>all disorders arising from impure blood or a deranged liver.</u> It's especially effective on <u>pimples, diabetes, or internal</u>

slime fever. This special formula can even cure <u>sudden death.</u>
<u>There's no sore it will not heal, no pain it will not subdue.</u>

Jack knew these words. They weren't exactly the same, but close enough to recognize. Dr. Kingsbury used them to describe his own tonic. Jack's eyes scanned the page, faster now:

<u>If you are not feeling just right and cannot locate the trou-</u>
<u>ble, take this wonderful medication before it's too late. You</u>
<u>don't know what minute you may be overtaken by some dire</u>
<u>calamity.</u>

Dr. Kingsbury had taken another man's words and claimed them as his own.

At the door, a movement caught Jack's eye. He shoved the book back on the shelf and quickly blew out the candles.

The doctor kicked the stool aside. He had to stoop to enter the wagon. "Jack? Are you in here? What are you doing?"

"I thought it might be cooler inside, so I . . ."

Smoke curled above the candlewicks. He glanced from the desk to the jars to the shelf. Had he left anything out of place?

"You didn't touch anything, did you?"

"No!"

Dr. Kingsbury put his hands on his hips, his elbows jutting out to the sides. "Next time ask for permission. Do you understand?"

"I'm sorry," Jack said. "I won't do it again."

The doctor took his coin pouch from his coat and unlocked the drawer in his desk. The pouch the doctor said Isaac had emptied. In the drawer Jack was never to touch.

"I've just talked to Mr. Brindley. If all goes as planned, we should have bottles and notices tomorrow afternoon. There'll be plenty of work for the two of us soon. Why don't you take those pennies I gave you and buy a treat while you've got the chance?"

Since they'd come to Oakdale four days ago, they'd had nothing but fish. Sunday night, Jack hadn't eaten at all. He remembered the wonderful smells from the bakery. Maybe they sold pie by the slice. He could almost taste the buttery crust, its soft center gooey with berries.

"Go on," Dr. Kingsbury said.

Jack made for the road, Bear at his heels, relieved the doctor hadn't asked more.

A FRIEND

THERE IT WAS. That voice again. Jack looked up from his carving, but the graveyard was empty—only silent rows of stones.

Bear lifted his head. He'd heard it, too.

Jack pushed the carving back into his pocket and stood in Memory's shadow. Her arms stretched above in silent comfort, an offering to those who grieved. He looked down the rows of stones, tracing the circular path. He'd been wrong; he wasn't alone. A dark-headed girl sat on the bench where Cora had told the oak's story.

It had to be her. "Come, Bear," he said.

Cora's brown eyes brightened when he approached. "Jack! I hoped I'd see you again."

"Were you talking to someone?"

"No," she said, her cheeks reddening.

"I thought I heard something. Never mind." Jack sat down beside her. Though his wrist was no longer swollen, a deep bruise spread over his skin. He tugged at his sleeve, making sure it was covered.

Cora twisted the toe of her boot in the grass, till she'd left a hole beneath her. "What are you doing here?"

He'd been sure the doctor would punish him when he'd been found in the wagon. But instead, Dr. Kingsbury had sent him to town. Jack had waited in line at the bakery, set to buy a slice of pie. Once he'd reached for the coins in his pocket, buying the pie hadn't felt right. He'd mumbled something about changing his mind and had gone to the graveyard instead. "Mostly I came here to think."

How the tonic's cure didn't come quickly for some. Why the doctor had stolen another man's words. What had happened to Isaac? Who was Ernest McPherson? A friend? Someone Isaac had met on the road?

"You were right," Cora said. "I was talking earlier." She gave an embarrassed smile. "To Robert Frasier, actually. Sometimes I come here to tell him things."

It made him feel special that she'd confessed, the sort of secret you offered a friend. "What were you talking to him about?"

"Nettie. My cousin. Yesterday she threatened to tell that

I went to the grove after school. She was upset when she saw me there. I don't know what made her so mad." Cora slammed the toe of her boot on the ground, breaking loose a divot of earth. "She didn't even want to go."

The dog placed his chin in Cora's lap. She stiffened and pushed it away. "It's okay, Cora. Bear's just being friendly."

"Bear?"

The dog turned.

"I've named him," Jack said. "I figured no one else had. Look." Jack took the carving from his pocket. He hadn't shown anyone since Isaac had left.

Cora traced the curve of its tail. "It's Bear, isn't it? He's got the same ears."

Jack smiled. She could tell what he was trying to make, and he wasn't even half done. "It's for Lucy."

"She'll love it." Cora paused. "Is it hard, being away from her?"

Jack nodded. No one loved him like Lu. She cried for him when she fell down. When the dark frightened her, it was Jack she wanted. Even when she'd been so sick, Lucy had only asked for him. When he got home, he'd make it up to her, the time that they'd lost while he was gone.

"I remembered something I wanted to tell you."

Cora leaned closer. "What is it?"

"Brandywine Falls. It's another place I saw." Jack wanted

to impress this girl. He'd tried to think what he might tell her so he had reason to see her again.

"Brandywine Falls. Where's that? What's it like?"

"North of Akron. Not too far away. It's a waterfall set back in the woods. Water cascades from a steep wall of rocks. It goes on and on and on."

Cora closed her eyes, considering. "Maybe I could see it one day."

"I hope you can. There's nothing else like it."

"Oh! I almost forgot," Cora said. "There's something I wanted to tell you, too. When I left the grove yesterday, I stopped by a place Nettie and I used to explore, an old abandoned farm. Someone bought it, a man with a silvery beard. He told me I could call him Silas. He's building a barn. I helped him a bit. You had so many questions about Oakdale. I thought you'd like to know."

A warm feeling spread through his chest. When he'd been thinking of Cora, she'd thought of him, too. "I tried to learn more about the tonic. I'm not quite sure what to make of it."

"What do you mean, you're not quite sure?"

"How it works," Jack said, "how it makes people better. So I went in the wagon when the doctor was gone and looked through some of his things."

Cora's eyes widened. "You did?"

Something wasn't quite right with the tonic. He wanted to tell her but wasn't sure how.

"I'm not even supposed to go in on my own. I looked through a couple of books, but I didn't find anything."

"Maybe you could ask the doctor."

Jack shook his head. He couldn't do that.

With her boot, she smoothed over the hole in the ground. "Have you gotten some of your thinking done?"

"A little, I guess." Jack had come to the graveyard to make sense of things, but mainly he'd only thought up more questions. If something was off with the tonic, how had Lu gotten better? How had it fixed Mr. Kennedy's ear?

Slowly, Cora reached for the dog and brushed her fingers over his head. "Bear. That's your name, is it?"

Jack could have sworn the dog smiled. He reached out his hand to stroke Bear's back.

"Oh." Cora's voice was soft. "Jack, what happened to you?"

His heart quickened as he saw his bruised wrist jutting from his sleeve. "I fell. Near the river." The lie came without prompting. He couldn't tell Cora what had happened, even though he wanted to.

"I'm sorry. That must have hurt."

"It really wasn't so bad." He wanted to tell her the

doctor had done it. Jack glanced at his wrist, the bruises still tender.

"I hope it's better soon."

"Cora," he said, "there's going to be another show. Four days from now, on Saturday. Do you think you could come? I've promised I'll tell Lucy's story and last time . . ." He didn't want to say out loud what a disaster last time had been.

"I'll be there." She inched closer, near enough their shoulders touched. "If it helps, you can pretend we're here on this bench, and you're telling Lu's story to me."

Cora was so easy to be with. Just knowing she'd come on Saturday gave Jack a measure of courage.

"I'd better go. I'll see you then." She trailed her fingers over the gravestone. "Bye, Uncle Robert," she said.

Jack read what was chiseled there:

ROBERT FRASIER

FOUNDER

FAITHFUL HUSBAND

FATHER

FRIEND

He watched as Cora ran down the path. Jack wasn't the sort to have many friends. Back home, he fished with a couple of boys. There was Lu, of course, but she was family. There was Isaac, but he was gone.

From the gate, Cora waved.

Jack raised his hand.

Now there was Cora Brindley.

A LESSON INTERRUPTED

CORA TUCKED HER chin as Nettie brushed past, pretending to study her lesson. She pulled her reader a little lower, making sure her journal couldn't be seen. Two days ago, Nettie had threatened to tell on her. For two days, they hadn't spoken. Since Monday, Cora had stayed in from recess and eaten her dinner alone.

"You missed the clouds," Nettie announced. "Everyone says it's going to rain."

Cora turned in her desk so her back was to Nettie. She'd had her fill of Nettie James.

"Fine," Nettie said. "Keep ignoring me." She put her dinner pail under her seat. "I didn't even tell your mother."

"Because you haven't had the chance."

The rest of the students filed in, bringing with them the heat. "Please continue on with your lessons," Mr. Ogden said. He stayed near the window, his eyes fixed outside.

The old Mr. Ogden wouldn't have wasted a day on boring book lessons. He wouldn't have drifted about like those distant clouds in the sky.

The room grew quiet as everyone settled, still enough to hear the creak of a bench as somebody shifted, the steady tick of the clock.

Nettie whispered to Cora's back, "You're acting ridiculous."

"I don't want to talk about it."

Mr. Ogden left the window and started down the farthest row, helping students who needed assistance.

Cora pulled her book closer. She'd forget about Nettie, starting this minute. Cora turned back a page in her journal, where she'd written about yesterday's meeting with Jack. For Oakdale's roots to stay deep and secure, strangers could visit, but they couldn't stay long. It was best to keep distant. Those were the rules. Cora had heard them most of her life.

What she hadn't known until a few days ago was how strongly she disagreed.

She touched the words on the page, uncertain if they were true. *Dr. Kingsbury might have hurt Jack.* He'd said he'd fallen, but the marks on his wrist didn't look right. They'd reminded her of long, delicate fingers.

Behind her, Mr. Ogden crouched near Janie's desk, a ruler poking from his back pocket. He was one row over from her own. Nettie picked up her slate and scribbled something, as if she'd not used her lesson time glaring but had been working all along. She tapped Cora's shoulder once Mr. Ogden moved on and held up the slate so Cora could read:

If you don't want to talk, then I'll tell Mr. Ogden.

Cora narrowed her eyes. "About what?"

Nettie erased the slate, trying not to smile. "About Monday," she whispered. "On the nature walk. How you wanted to spy on the doctor's wagon. Or I could tell him you're not doing lessons but writing in that book."

Cora lifted the top of her desk, but she wasn't quick enough. Nettie lunged from her seat and grabbed the journal before Cora could put it away.

"Girls." Mr. Ogden stood in front of them, only three desks away. "What's going on?"

"Nothing." Nettie was pure sweetness. She waited for him to pass on. "Let's see." Nettie opened the cover.

Cora shot to her feet. "How dare you. That's mine!"

"Miss Brindley." Mr. Ogden turned back. His tone held a warning.

"Give that back!"

"Cora," he said, "kindly take your seat."

"I don't know what's upset her," Nettie insisted. She held up empty hands.

"That's not true, Nettie James, and you know it." Nettie had shoved the journal under her seat; Cora had seen her do it. She could act like nothing had happened, but Cora refused to lie.

The whole room was still. Everyone stared. Cora couldn't say Nettie had taken her journal. That would prove she hadn't been doing her work.

"Sit down, young lady. Do it now."

"No," Cora said, planting her feet.

He yanked the ruler from his pocket. It bit into her hand with a snap.

Mr. Ogden had hit her!

The room was a blur of startled faces.

"Go outside." He flung his arm at the door. "Stay there until you've calmed yourself down."

She stomped across the room and yanked the door open, hard enough it hit the wall. Outside, the breeze blustered. Angry. Hot. A red strip blazed the back of her hand.

HOLD TO HOPE

MR. OGDEN SAT on the schoolhouse steps, his gaze set on the sky. Sweat drenched his shirt and his forearms had reddened. The steady breeze cooled him a little, but he wouldn't move away from the heat. He didn't deserve the shaded porch. Not after the damage he'd done.

Cora Brindley had left. Without word. With no warning. That was what he'd told himself at first. But the longer he witnessed the swelling clouds climb, he'd realized it wasn't the truth.

He'd used the ruler on one of his students. That was the heart of the problem. He'd hurt and humiliated Cora. How had he let himself do it? Mr. Ogden had always kept order at school. In all his years teaching, this was the only time he'd ever hit anyone. Not many teachers could say the same.

He prided himself on being considerate. He listened to his students and helped when he could. His first obligation was to enliven young minds, and he had been negligent of late. How long had it been since he'd recommended a book he'd known Cora would like? When was the last time he'd set aside lessons and invited his students to dream? There'd been the nature walk, two days ago, but even then he'd been consumed with himself.

With the palsy and the tonic.

Mr. Ogden wiped his face with his cuff. He rested his hands on his knees. While his fingers on the left pulsed, those on the right stayed calm. He'd started the medicine Saturday evening. That was four days back. Every morning since then, he'd taken it faithfully. Yet there'd been no shift in his symptoms, not one. If he'd been told Saturday that he'd still be waiting, he wouldn't have believed it.

Mr. Ogden stood and tested his foot. It didn't tighten or tense. For the length of the schoolyard, he walked without worry. Perhaps the medicine would do its work sooner if he returned to his usual morning walks. He loved wandering through town in the early light, but for weeks he'd kept his exercise short, leaving home in the dark so he wouldn't be seen.

During school, he shielded himself with his desk. At church, he took the last pew after service started and left before the closing hymn. He'd turned down a chance to see friends in Greenville and three supper invitations.

Because no one could know he had taken ill. It would cost him his job. The last teacher was proof of that. It was as if he'd pulled a curtain closed to protect himself from notice. But the curtain that kept him separate also held him back. It blocked him from the life he enjoyed. It shut him off from his students.

What had happened wasn't Cora's failing but his own.

Nettie hadn't said much when he'd questioned her, but he'd pieced together enough to follow. The girls had quarreled. Cora said Nettie had taken something, but when Mr. Ogden had checked Nettie's desk, he hadn't found anything.

The cousins were close, but they sometimes bickered. They'd be friends again soon. It was his job to apologize to Cora. He would make things right in the morning.

The clouds drifted, obscuring the sun. It was time to set his worries aside. Tomorrow he'd increase his tonic dose and set his focus back on his students. This afternoon he'd get to work on that history the school board had asked him to write. He had an idea he wanted to explore, but first he'd need it approved by one of the trustees.

Everything would come together. He must hold to that hope.

Mr. Ogden quickened his pace. His stride was strong with no wavering steps.

What he had to do was believe.

CLOUDS AND FIRE

"NANA?" CORA PEEKED around the half-open door. "May I come in?"

Nana rocked in her chair near the darkened window, a candle her only companion. Outside, tree branches stirred in the breeze, a breeze that hadn't let up since morning.

"Nana?"

This time her grandmother turned. "Cora, how nice to see you. Come, sit with me."

Cora scooted a chair across the floor so that she, too, faced the window. She wasn't sure what Nana saw, but whatever it was, it kept her attention. Candlelight danced on the windowpane. Shadow branches shifted outside. Cora tried to settle into the silence.

Mr. Ogden was downstairs with Father. He'd knocked on the door a few minutes ago. She traced the mark on her hand with her fingers. At supper she'd tried to keep it hidden. She'd run from the schoolhouse, unsure where to go, run far enough so that no one would ask why she wasn't in school. Cora had wandered the outskirts of town and had ended up near McCalls'. Silas had been in the field, putting up his barn. She'd stayed and helped for a while, holding boards steady as he nailed them in place. Silas was kind. Cora enjoyed his company. She'd found herself telling him more about Jack: The lighthouse he'd seen on Lake Erie's shore. The waterfall with its slick rock wall. How Jack wasn't scared of the old stray dog, and Cora had bravely petted it, too.

"Upstairs, Cora," Father had said when he'd let Mr. Ogden in. She'd lingered on the steps, hoping to catch what they were saying, but Mother had sent her to Nana's room.

Of course he'd come. Because of what had happened.

"Do you mind if I open the window a little?" Even after the sun had set, the heat was still unbearable.

The rocker eased back and forth. "Not at all, my dear."

Cora cracked the window open. The breeze washed over her, cool and inviting.

"Rain's coming soon," Nana said.

Nettie had said the same earlier. Was Nana watching the clouds through the black? Oakdale certainly needed rain, but Cora wasn't convinced it was coming. The clouds had been wrong before, like the day Dr. Kingsbury arrived.

"This summer's been so terribly hot." The rocker went on with its creaking.

"It's fall now, Nana," Cora said. "But you're right, it feels like summer."

"Hasn't rained in an age. I hope we don't have another fire."

"A fire?" Cora couldn't remember a fire since the blaze at the bakery a few years ago, but that had been snuffed out quickly.

"Like the fire at McCalls'. You remember, don't you? The months of drought. The thundering horses. The barn burning with light."

Cora knew of no fire. Mr. McCall had died years ago. She'd never seen a barn there before Silas had started building his own.

Nana clasped her hands in her lap. "There was talk someone set it. The boy got the blame."

It must be one of Nana's memories, something that had happened long ago. "Who was the boy?" Cora asked.

"Not someone from Oakdale. A boy with eyes like the stars."

Cora couldn't imagine how that might look. Nana must be confused, her mind not right.

Downstairs a door closed. Cora went to the window

and pushed it wide. She saw Mr. Ogden walking home, an odd hitch in his gait. She could leave Nana's room now that he was gone, but she wasn't sure she was ready.

"Is the air too much?" Cora asked.

Nana smiled. "I'm fine."

It was probably time for Cora to go. Nana needed her rest. "Good night," she said and kissed Nana's cheek.

"I said the boy wasn't the one, but no one in town believed me. Then they put up that fence to keep strangers out."

Cora stopped near the door.

"What did I know? I was only a girl. That's what everyone said. But I'd seen the horses run from the flames. The boy drove them out of the barn."

The story of the fire again. While Nana had seemed muddled before, now Cora was certain her mind was quite sound. "What do you mean, you were only a girl?"

"I wasn't supposed to be outside, but sometimes I slipped out to watch the moon rise." Candlelight brightened Nana's face. Though wrinkles fanned from her brown eyes, Cora could picture the girl she'd once been. "That night, the moon called to me, round and bright and lovely. I sat on the fence at the edge of our field, the one that bordered McCalls'."

The moon and stars. The clouds with their patterns.

Others seldom watched the skies, but Nana had always admired their beauty.

"If the boy set the fire as they said he did, he'd have no need to escape. He'd have run long before the fire took hold."

Cora knelt before her grandmother. The chair came to a stop. She'd heard of a fire in Oakdale's past. It had burned the north side of town and stopped at the Great Oak Tree. Could this be the same one? "Who was the boy?" Cora asked. Someone who wasn't from Oakdale, Nana had said. A boy who'd caught trouble when he wasn't to blame.

Nana reached for Cora's hands. "My mind doesn't work the way it once did. I can't remember his name."

"Tell me the story," Cora said. She wanted to hear the memory with its danger and boy and drought.

Nana leaned back and shut her eyes. "Mornings I often sat on the fence, watching the sun pink the fields with its rising. Sometimes a boy passed by. I called out to him. He didn't say much, mostly kept to himself, but each day he stayed a little longer. One morning gray clouds streaked the skies. 'Looks like rain,' he said, 'but don't expect any.' And wouldn't you know?" Nana said. "That evening, the skies rumbled and gleamed, but though it tried, the rain never fell. It was months before the drought finally ended."

The rocker started again with its creaking.

"We became friends, the two of us. He was thoughtful and gentle and kind. A boy like that wouldn't start a fire. Even if I hadn't seen him escape, I would have been certain he wasn't the one. But what did I know? I was only a child."

It was unfair, what happened sometimes. Like the smack of a ruler. Nana's struggling mind. And how quickly the words of a girl were ignored. Like the fate of a boy who'd gotten the blame for a fire long ago.

"I believe you, Nana," Cora said. It meant little after so many years, but she told Nana anyhow. "Even if you were a child then, I believe what you saw."

AN EXTRA MEASURE

"LIKE THIS." DR. Kingsbury drew a long breath. "Feel the air run deep to your middle."

Wind stirred the willow branches. The tang of newly mixed tonic drifted from the wagon. It was Friday, the day before the show, and Jack felt like he'd never be ready.

He inhaled until his lungs ached.

"Now tilt your chin upward. Make your voice bold, strong enough to reach everyone."

Isaac had started every show with a flash of fiery speech. Jack wouldn't be able to do half as well. He shut his eyes and gave it his best. "Dr. Kingsbury's medicine—"

"Too gentle. Try it again."

Confidence like Isaac's. That's what he needed.

"Dr. Kingsbury's Medicine Show." Jack's words were powerful at first, but the rest came out in a rush. "Find answers, gain hope, discover healing."

"No, no." Dr. Kingsbury frowned. "Say it slower this time. The crowd must feel the weight of your words."

There was so much to learn and plenty of ways to muddle things without even trying. This was something Jack had to get right. He couldn't have the doctor angry again.

Dr. Kingsbury sat on the wagon's steps. "Let's try this. Tell me about the pie you bought a few days ago. How did it taste? What did it smell like? Pick words that make me want to go buy some."

"It was good," Jack said too quickly. The unspent pennies weighed down his pocket. "I mean, it was fine. Not as good as at home but . . ." His face reddened. Why had he lied?

Dr. Kingsbury sighed. "Slow down. You're rushing again. Let every sentence do its work." The doctor's dark eyes settled on Jack. "Now tell me again. This time with meaning."

"It was good. Very tasty. The blueberries were . . ." Surely the doctor knew Jack was fibbing. This had to be some kind of test. "The crust . . ." Jack couldn't go on.

"You've got to practice for this to work. Tomorrow, you'll have to convince the audience that what you're saying is true. Tell me. How did the tonic cure your sister?"

Jack knew every detail of Lucy's recovery. At night, when he couldn't sleep, remembering her healing comforted him. Each change he'd seen had been an assurance she'd be healthy again. "The medicine brought her fever down. It took the rattle from her chest."

"Those are the facts," Dr. Kingsbury said. "Now turn them into a story. That's what makes people see. Let it build as you draw your listeners in. When it peaks, prick their hearts with emotion. You must speak of your pain, but don't linger there. Always end with an offer of hope. That's what binds people together. It's a powerful medicine all its own, a promise of better days. When hardship comes, hope keeps a soul going."

It was hope that had driven Jack to the show the first time he'd seen the doctor. That morning, over a year ago, Mrs. Anderson had knocked at their door. She'd brought a cake on a blue-patterned dish. Mrs. Anderson was like a granny to him, a kindly old neighbor who visited often. "How's your Lucy faring?" she asked.

"About the same." The warm smell of cake made Jack's stomach clench. He hadn't eaten all morning. He showed Mrs. Anderson to the parlor, where Papa had moved Lucy's bed. A fire burned in the hearth, despite the summer heat. Lucy lay sleeping nearby, wrapped in a woolen blanket.

Jack stayed in the doorway. It didn't feel right, going in.

When Ma saw Mrs. Anderson, she covered her face and wept. Jack's hunger was swallowed up by dread. Not once since Lucy had taken sick had he seen his mother cry.

"Now, now. It will be all right." Mrs. Anderson put an arm around her.

"It won't," Ma said. "She's not getting better."

"Martha, listen to me. There's a man visiting town. Kingsbury's his name. He's a doctor whose tonic cures most anything. My Charlie saw his medicine show."

Ma wiped her eyes with Mrs. Anderson's handkerchief.

"I couldn't help but think of your Lucy." The fire crackled, the flames leaping high. "You know how Bertie Simpson suffers from shortness of breath. Well, the doctor gave Bertie some of his tonic. How Bertie puckered, my Charlie said—must have tasted awful going down— but would you believe it? Bertie Simpson perked up right quick. He was able to breathe, deep and steady. His haggard expression faded away, that's what my Charlie said!"

Mr. Simpson had always been weak, a man worn down by everyday living. If this doctor had healed Mr. Simpson, maybe his medicine could also help Lucy.

Jack had to find Dr. Kingsbury.

"Ma?" he said as he entered the room. "I'll go see that doctor, if you'd like."

"Oh, Jack. We don't have any extra money."

He reached for her hand. "Let me go. Don't you worry. I'll make sure Lucy gets what she needs. You go lie down for a bit. I'm sure Mrs. Anderson will sit with Lu."

He surprised himself with what he'd said. Mrs. Anderson hadn't offered to stay. Jack had never told Ma what to do before. The news of the tonic had made him brave.

"I'd be happy to watch her," Mrs. Anderson said. "Come now, Martha. Let's get you some rest."

"Wait." Ma's gray eyes peered up at Jack. For a moment it felt like he was the grown-up and his mother was the child. "Thank you for caring for Lucy like this."

Every part of him hoped the tonic would work. Was that what had made Lucy better? The tonic or his belief in it?

Dr. Kingsbury pushed back a lock of hair. "You trusted the tonic would heal your sister. Not everyone has the same faith. Some have a hope so strong, the tonic is a quick remedy. Others have been brought very low, so low, they need time for their faith to strengthen. You understand, don't you, Jack?"

It made a certain kind of sense. Some people needed more than one show to help them believe. Yesterday he'd hung new handbills in town:

WHATEVER THE AILMENT, DR. KINGSBURY'S
MIRACULOUS TONIC IS THE CURE.

Hear the Story of a Remarkable
Healing in Oakdale.

Learn of a Sick Child's Complete
and Total Recovery.

Come One, Come All!
Whatever Your Need,
Elijah Kingsbury Has the Answers.

§

SATURDAY IN FOUNDER'S SQUARE
AT THREE O'CLOCK.

"Those who struggle and doubt, they're the ones who need a doctor's care most. What kind of doctor would I be if I didn't provide for them?" Dr. Kingsbury took something from his pocket and handed it to Jack. "Have a look. I had it printed in Greenville earlier this week. For customers who need their hope restored."

It was a label meant for the bottles. Jack read it twice, but it still made no sense:

Dr. Kingsbury's Improved Miraculous Tonic
Relieves Every Malady Known to Man or Beast

"I've made a new formula. Think of it, Jack. Comfort and hope for those who need it. A steal for only five cents more."

Something inside Jack turned, as though he'd just smelled spoiled milk. On the surface, nothing looked different between a fresh cup and milk that had soured. But one whiff was all you needed to know a cup of milk had gone bad.

The doctor had lied to Mr. Ogden. He'd stolen Dr. Kilmer's words. He claimed faith bolstered the tonic: The stronger it was, the more potent the medicine.

Jack didn't believe what the doctor was saying. There couldn't be a new formula. He would have washed the tonic pot twice—once for the first batch and once for the second. But he'd taken it down the river one time. And wouldn't the doctor need days, maybe weeks, to test a new recipe?

"The old formula is on the shelves. The new tonic is in a crate near the door. You'll need to label all of the bottles. Just think of it. With your work, you're offering hope to those who battle uncertainty. You're giving an extra measure of faith—the kind that might lead to a healing like Lucy's."

These new labels weren't only to comfort; they were meant to deceive. They were meant to lure the hopeless in, trick them into thinking their problems were solved.

Jack sat on the wagon's steps and rested his head on his knees. He'd trusted Dr. Kingsbury. He'd believed everything the doctor claimed. He'd thought he was part of something good, selling cures in a bottle in every town where they'd stopped. Even if the doctor had a temper, even though he sometimes was rough, Jack had believed he was a well-meaning healer. But lately, that had started to change. The lies. The stolen words. The stolen words. Dr. Kingsbury bent the truth to suit his needs. At first, Jack had made excuses for the doctor, but not any longer.

He was done with that.

THE SECOND SHOW

DR. KINGSBURY TAPPED his wrist. It was three o'clock.

In the shade of the oak, people had gathered, a far bigger crowd than the week before. Jack filled his lungs as the doctor had taught him. He'd get through this; there was no other choice. "Ladies and gentlemen. Boys and girls. Welcome to Dr. Kingsbury's Show!"

Yesterday, after he'd pasted the labels, he'd practiced his speech at the riverbank. He'd gone through it again this morning as he tried to ignore his growing unease.

Jack studied the crowd. Young and old, there had to be hundreds of them. The whole town, it seemed like. He spoke slowly, making sure not to rush. "If you long for hope, you are welcome here. Come, if you need to be healed. To-day we offer the balm your soul needs." The crowd pressed close. Jack raised his chin. "I give you the miracle worker himself, Dr. Elijah Kingsbury!"

Around him, voices rose to shouts. The first part was over. There was still more to come. Jack perched on the wagon's steps, his heart wildly beating.

Dr. Kingsbury lifted his hands like a man who brought the glories of heaven. His black suit was newly pressed. A fresh poppy adorned his buttonhole. "Thank you, people of Oakdale, for joining me a second time!"

The doctor opened the cupboard door and turned to face the crowd. "In the week since I arrived in town, I've had dozens of customers come to the grove. They can attest to what I now tell you." He paced as he spoke, so all might hear. "Miraculous, that's what I call my tonic. Why, you might ask? Because it surpasses all other medicines."

There they were. Dr. Kilmer's words. Jack could still see them on the book's worn pages.

"It heals disorders of impure blood. It treats upset stomachs and calms riotous livers. Use it to soothe pimples or rashes. If you suffer from diabetes or heart complica-tions, my tonic is the cure. There's no sore it will not heal, no pain it will not subdue. If you are not feeling right and cannot locate the trouble, take my wonderful medicine. You don't know what minute you may be overtaken by some dire calamity." The doctor paused. "And if you're concerned about your life's end, my tonic can even cure sudden death!"

"Prove it!" a person called from the back. "Prove your medicine does those things." Through the crowd stormed the man with gingered whiskers, the one who'd badgered Jack last Saturday. Mr. Mueller, that's what Cora had called him. He pushed past the people in the front of the crowd, his face angry and red.

"Tobias. Calm yourself down." Mayor James caught the man's sleeve.

Mr. Mueller snatched his arm away.

"Tobias Mueller," the mayor said. "Please."

Reluctantly, the man moved aside, his eyes still trained on the doctor.

Dr. Kingsbury showed no concern for the outburst. "Here's all the proof you need." He called to the crowd: "Who here has experienced the tonic's effects?"

A scattering of people raised their hands.

"You," the doctor said to a woman, "tell everyone what the tonic has done."

She swayed, a child at her hip, staring Mr. Mueller down. "It's comforted our teething baby. Tobias, why are you acting like this? You've seen our boy change. You know it's true."

"A coincidence," Mr. Mueller said.

"And you?" Dr. Kingsbury pointed to a man who stood near the oak.

"It took the sting out of poison ivy."

"It's helped with my rheumatism," Mrs. Kennedy offered. "My fingers fairly fly when I'm sewing."

The doctor nodded, satisfied.

"Look around. See your neighbors and friends. For some, the tonic has only begun to reveal its miraculous power. For others, their lives were transformed so quickly, they'll be never the same." He turned to the wagon. "Like my assistant, Jack." The doctor motioned for Jack to come forward.

Jack fought the urge to look at the sky, the ground, the oak—anywhere but at the people in front of him. His story was true, but the hope he offered was twisted and tainted now.

"I have a sister named Lucy." The sound of his voice jarred his ears. He swallowed and pushed ahead. "Last year, she came down with a fever."

The first show, he'd made it no further than this. His face flushed as he realized words had escaped him. He wasn't sure how to continue. *Turn your facts to a story,* the doctor had taught him. *Draw your listeners in.* All that practice he'd done, what good would it be? He planned to knowingly lie to these people.

A girl moved from the edge of the crowd. Cora. He couldn't have missed her. Jack met her eyes, gentle and calm. He could do this. True or not, he could tell everyone what had happened to Lucy.

"My mother tried everything, but Lucy got worse. Then our neighbor told us about Dr. Kingsbury, a doctor who was visiting town. I hurried to his medicine show. He said his tonic could hold back death." Jack's throat tightened, but he kept on going. "I couldn't lose my little sister, but my family had no money to spare. Dr. Kingsbury, he gave me a bottle for free. Ma had Lu take a dose. By supper, she was hungry for the first time in weeks."

Jack slowed, his eyes lingering on the crowd. They were, all of them, taken in.

"In the morning her fever was gone."

The more he'd thought about the tonic, the more he'd come back to this: Maybe the medicine hadn't healed Lucy. Maybe what Lu had needed was time. Time for her fever to break. Time for her body to heal on its own.

Applause burst around him, pulsed under his skin.

He'd done it. He'd told Lucy's story. Now people trusted the tonic had healed Lucy. They assumed Jack believed in the doctor when he didn't anymore.

Dr. Kingsbury rested his hand on Jack's shoulder. "There's been another miraculous healing, this one here in town. On Monday, Mayor James asked for this show, so everyone might hear the man's story. Henry Graham, please make your way to the front."

Whispers awakened in the hush as an elderly man came forward.

ONE OF THEM

SILAS SHADED HIS eyes from the glaring sun. There was Henry. In fifty-one years, Silas hadn't forgotten him. As the man hobbled by, the crowd parted like waves, as the Red Sea had done in Bible times. Henry limped through its middle, his hair grizzled and body bowed.

Though Henry's chin jutted forward and his face ran to wrinkles, Silas saw the boy with the wheat-colored hair. The boy who'd played his little tricks. Who'd heaped blame on Silas when the fire had started till there wasn't a chance folks hadn't believed.

Silas's palms burned, like an itch settling in. He'd figured when he'd come back to Oakdale, he'd see Henry, if the man was still living. It was only a matter of time. Silas had every right to be here, as much as Henry Graham. So why was it he felt like a child again, falsely accused and alone?

"Welcome," the doctor said, once Henry reached him. "Please tell us your remarkable story."

Henry Graham cleared his throat, his voice dry and feeble. "John Hicks." He coughed and tried again. "John bought some tonic Monday morning. He used it for a rash on his arm, a rash that healed up quick. He figured the tonic might do me some good, maybe ease the ache in my leg. The first time I tried it, nothing happened except for a coughing fit. That tonic of yours, Dr. Kingsbury, it's got quite the burn when you swallow it."

The doctor smiled. "Medicine is never meant to taste good."

"I tried it again a few hours later, though John said to take it once a day." Henry glanced upward. "Sorry, Doc. That second time, a tingling started in my heel and spread over my foot. I needed to walk—that's the best way to describe it. I picked up my crutch, but not for long. At first, I didn't make it far. Just from my parlor to the front porch. It wasn't easy, I still limped a bit, but never since I was a boy had I walked without any help. I let myself rest a little, then my foot took to itching again. I knew I had to get up and get moving. This time I made it down the steps and all the way to the end of the street. The Thompsons saw.

The Kennedys, too. Soon folks were opening their doors, amazed at my passing. 'It's that tonic!' I told them. 'I've been cured from my crutch.'"

In the days after the fire, Henry and Bill and Ray had stayed away from McCalls'. They'd gathered most of the wheat they could salvage, but Silas kept on, burdened with the last of the work. When the boys returned, when the rumors started, Henry had come to the farm with a crutch. Said he'd caught his foot in a rabbit's burrow, but he hadn't said when or where.

Silas had pictured Henry running, through the dark, past the fields, till he'd reached the woods—McCalls' barn burning behind him. Maybe he'd twisted his foot then, as he'd taken off after setting the fire.

Silas had no proof, of course, but he'd gotten the job, not Henry's brother. What better way to get back at McCall and the boy who had taken his brother's position?

Henry set his eyes on the crowd. "I'm never going back to that crutch. Not now. Not ever."

That was a shame, Silas thought. The man could get around on his own if he took his steps careful and slow. Could be his limp had improved, but it wasn't entirely gone. It wouldn't do him any harm to use his crutch now and again.

"And you'll never need to," Dr. Kingsbury said, "if you keep to regular doses of tonic. Imagine how strong your leg will be a few more weeks from now." He led the man to a three-legged stool. "Please make yourself comfortable, Mr. Graham. You've earned yourself a rest."

What was the doctor thinking, bringing everyone out in the heat? Were they here just to watch an old man limp, or was there something more?

Something about the doctor was off. Silas had known since that day in the store. It was more than healing the doctor was after. Could be money or high opinion. They would feed a man hungry for fame. The doctor had won over Mr. Brindley. He had the support of Mayor James, too.

The doctor's boy stood in the shadows. His too-big britches hung at his waist. He was a boy like Silas had been. In need of some money. Out of place. Beholden to the man who employed him. Befriended by a girl in town.

This boy had been left to the doctor's mercy. Whatever the doctor had planned, the boy would bear the consequence.

When Dr. Kingsbury healed that man's ear, some people had been taken in, but not everyone. A new miracle could win a crowd over. Healing a man of his need for a crutch could turn the doubters into those who believed.

CALL THE WIND

MR. GRAHAM SHUFFLED slowly as he found his seat. Cora didn't know what to make of it. Ever since she'd known him, he'd used a crutch, and here he was walking on his own.

The crowd that had gathered in the square was much larger than the week before. Cora saw Reverend Wells and his family, Mr. and Mrs. Kennedy, and every one of the Thompson kids—their curly heads in a row. Cuthbert ran past with a group of boys and found his place beside Uncle Nathanael. But no Nettie. She wasn't there.

It had been three days since their argument. Cora had been certain Father would punish her, but he'd said nothing that night when she'd left Nana's room. On Thursday morning, before class began, Mr. Ogden had pulled her aside with Nettie. He'd asked them to apologize. At first, Cora thought she was meant to say sorry for sassing and disrupting the class. But Mr. Ogden made her face Nettie and told her to look in her cousin's eyes. "Tell Nettie you're sorry," he'd said. Cora had mumbled something or other. Nettie had apologized, too, but neither of them meant any of it. Until she got her journal back, Cora refused to forgive.

Then Mr. Ogden had asked Cora's forgiveness for getting angry and hitting her. It had taken Cora aback. When had a grown-up ever done that?

Dr. Kingsbury took a bottle from his pocket. "This is the tonic that helped Henry Graham and restored Jack's little sister." Wind shook loose the poppy tucked in his buttonhole. It drifted to the ground. "In twelve years of travel, the tonic's cured hundreds, but even I am sometimes surprised at the miracles my medicine works."

A gust of wind rocked the oak. The old story said its limbs had unfurled that winter long ago. It was Oakdale's first miracle, a testament to Uncle Robert's constant care. Now Mr. Kennedy had been healed. Mr. Graham had grown stronger and could walk on his own. Two miracles in Oakdale a few days apart. How had it happened? Jack wasn't sure about the tonic, but he'd told Lucy's story just the same.

The doctor drew the cork from the bottle with a

satisfying pop. "It's no secret that Oakdale longs for rain. Wells have gone dry. Crops have withered. If the ground could cry out, it would beg for a drink. But take heart, my friends. Change is coming. Days ago, a breeze stirred the air. That breeze built to a steady wind. The wind ushered in the gathering clouds."

As one, the crowd looked overhead. It was true. The sky was full of them.

"Do you know what brought the change?" The doctor held the bottle aloft, like a man with a candle in a darkened room. "Dr. Kingsbury's Miraculous Tonic. It has the power to call the wind and draw forth the teeming clouds.

"Monday afternoon, a man came to the grove and told me a curious story. Earlier that day, he'd taken a dose and left his bottle uncorked near a window."

Cora had seen a bottle like that, in the window of Father's store.

"That was the day of the wakening winds. He encouraged his neighbors to try the same. That afternoon the clouds formed. The wind raised the clouds. Clouds lead to rain, and rain's what's sorely needed." The doctor stepped on the fallen poppy as he neared the crowd. "Do you want rain to return to Oakdale? Then buy a bottle of tonic."

The doctor's speech grew like a coming storm. "I implore you, people of Oakdale. Those who long for nourishing rain, who cherish this community. Do what's best. Do what's right. Act as Robert Frasier would have wanted. Put a bottle of tonic in every window. Bring back the rain for Founder's Day."

He lifted the bottle higher still. "For Robert Frasier!"

"For Robert Frasier!" the crowd said.

"For Oakdale!" Dr. Kingsbury shouted.

The voices around Cora roared in answer.

She felt a tug on her sleeve. Gray eyes peeked from behind jagged hair. Jack signaled her to follow.

Dr. Kingsbury called out as she hurried through the crowd. "If you long for healing, if you desire change, buy yourself a bottle. If you want what's best for your town, buy a second to bring on the rain. One for you. One for Oakdale."

Jack didn't stop until they reached the crowd's edge. "You can't believe him. I don't anymore."

"Come if you're riddled with failure," Dr. Kingsbury said. "Come if you're weighed down by doubts. There's no need to worry or be afraid. If you long for a remedy, come!"

As quick as he'd found her, Jack was gone. The crowd surged forward, eager for tonic, crushing the poppy under their feet.

A BOY'S DISAPPEARANCE

THE PLAY. THAT'S how Miss Moore knew the doctor. She stood in the middle of the churning crowd as the memory came through. The play was where she'd seen Kingsbury, if that was even his name. At home in Wabash. In City Park.

It must have been seven years back.

The whole town was abuzz when the troupe had arrived. A chain of painted wagons, half a dozen at least, had lined the road near the park. All summer the troupe performed Shakespeare's plays. She'd gone with her parents a number of times. It had all been so new and exciting. Miss Moore delighted in the beautiful costumes, their fabrics that shimmered like butterfly wings and a sunset's golden hues. She remembered the wild applause, the flicker of fireflies as the actors bowed. What a magical time it had been.

The line for the tonic coiled and grew. Miss Moore stepped out of its path. Really, the doctor's medicine show had stirred up quite a fuss.

Had it been seven years? That wasn't right. Seven summers ago, she'd been sick with the mumps. Six years, then. The summer she'd turned seventeen. The same summer Ernest McPherson went missing. He was a local boy, one year behind her in school. Ernest was the dependable sort who'd taken a job as a stagehand.

What a peculiar summer it had been. The newspaper was full of the boy's disappearance. There was speculation he'd up and left, but that didn't fit the Ernest she knew. Another story, a darker one, hinted he'd met with a sinister end. Poor Ernest. It was awful to consider.

As far as she knew, he'd never been found. Yet while many in town searched for him, life continued on. In City Park, people spread their blankets. Whispers hung in the evening air: Where could Ernest have gone? Would someone else disappear, too?

It had been a summer of beauty and joy. Worry and mystery. Next time Miss Moore wrote home, she'd ask if anything else had ever been learned about him.

The line for the tonic stretched from the wagon and circled around the oak. It reached the edge of Founder's Square and spilled onto the street. Wind tousled Kingsbury's hair, his unbroken attention set on his customers. Like a king before his countrymen, he was revered and adored. A person couldn't help but be drawn to him. That's what had given him away. He carried himself like he lived on the stage—that and the bottle of tonic. When he'd raised it high above his head, Miss Moore had remembered a rapier. A glimmer of metal. The clang of two swords.

The doctor and actor were one and the same.

That summer, Kingsbury had been exceptional. He'd been written up in the *Wabash Weekly*. Six years ago it had been, when the man said he'd been a doctor for twelve.

Had Ernest gotten mixed up with him?

Kingsbury was a fraud and a liar. So how was it his tonic had helped with her headaches, twice over now?

TRUTH AND STORIES

MANY LINGERED IN Founder's Square after the second medicine show. They talked as dusk fell, holding their bottles and wandering the streets long after dark. The air hummed with the trill of crickets. Stars sparked. Clouds swelled. Children long past their bedtimes danced in the square.

Silas witnessed it all.

The bottles of tonic were everywhere. Carried in baskets, in pockets, in bags. Passed hand to hand and lavished as gifts. A man opened a bottle and took a swig, as though he'd ordered a drink in the tavern. A woman washed her hands with a tonic-soaked cloth. Children emptied their bottles around the oak so the potion might nourish the tree.

Near the square, Henry Graham sat on a bench. Silas was surprised to find him alone. He'd thought a whole crowd might have swarmed the man with questions about his healing. Fear kindled inside Silas, as though the man still had a hold over him. He took a deep breath and let it out slowly. He wasn't a child anymore. That fear was something he had to let go.

As windowsills filled with tonic bottles, corks covered the sidewalks beneath. A man said why should they stop at windows? Why not doorways or fence posts or out in the street? If the tonic really could bring the rain, couldn't it do its work anyplace? Soon tonic bottles lined the sidewalks. Some set them on rooftops and hitching posts. A few even whispered of bottles set 'round the souls asleep in their graves.

"Evening," Silas said as he sat next to Henry.

"Bit of a strange one," Henry answered. He squeezed his ankle, like it gave him trouble. "The first time in hours I've had to myself."

Maybe that was a hint Silas should move on. Could be it was, but he wasn't leaving.

Not far from the oak, a group had gathered, many with lanterns in their hands. "Spread the word," a man at the front was saying. "The doctor has come to bring us rain!" The group broke apart, lantern lights bobbing, as they carried the message down the street.

Henry looked Silas over. "Are you new in town?"

Silas nodded. "I am."

Henry kept with his staring. "Have we met before?"

"A while back." *When we were boys. When you told folks I started the fire.* Silas breathed slow and deep. It wouldn't do to get angry now. "A long time ago. That summer at McCalls'."

Maybe it would have been best to keep quiet, but Silas knew secrets could eat at a man. He'd come back to Oakdale to make things right, to repair the wrongs done against him.

Henry's eyes hardened. "I remember you now. You're the boy who brought the drought."

It was interesting Henry didn't mention the fire. Perhaps he didn't want to remember what Silas suspected really happened that night. Henry, who'd made certain others blamed Silas. Who'd returned to work with a limp days after the barn had burned down.

Maybe pride kept Henry from using his crutch. He'd given it up in front of the town. Could be he felt there was no going back.

"That's not the way I remember it. There's truth and there's stories," Silas said. "It depends on what you believe."

GREENVILLE

IT WAS SUNDAY morning. Greenville's streets were deserted. Jack had left the grove early for the six-mile walk. Dr. Kingsbury never questioned how he spent his days off, as long as he was back before supper.

He had to find Isaac's cousin today. The problem was he wasn't sure how. Two weeks ago Isaac had paid her a visit. Jack hoped that's where Isaac was, here in Greenville with his cousin.

Leaves skittered across the cobblestones. Jack passed the empty train station and rows of shuttered shops. Greenville was the county seat, a place where people came to do business. The newspaper was printed here. It was home to the courthouse and sheriff's office. Beyond the brick buildings surrounding the square stood an old white wooden church. Children rushed out ahead of their families as the organ played its final notes.

"Excuse me," Jack said to the first man he saw. "I'm looking for a girl with the last name of Blum. Do you know where I could find her?"

The man held his hat against the wind. "I'm sorry," he said, "but that name's not familiar."

Jack tried with his question again and again, but the answers were the same. No one here knew Isaac's cousin.

He continued on, unsure what to do. Some boys ran by, kicking a ball, one with eyes the same blue as Isaac's. "Hold on!" Jack called. They slowed so he could catch up, but none of them knew a girl named Blum. The lights were on in the bakery, but when he knocked, no one answered the door. He could try the houses, but where would he start? If the *Greenville Journal* were open today, he could try to place an ad in the paper, though it had to cost more than his five pennies.

In front of the grocery, a man swept the steps. "Do you need something?" he asked Jack. The man was bald and big bellied, his arms thick and strong.

"I'm looking for someone. Her last name's Blum. Have you heard that name before?"

"Hmm. Can't say that I have."

"She's my friend's cousin. A few weeks ago, when we were in town, he stayed with her and—"

"Wait a moment." The man squinted at Jack. "I thought I'd seen you before. You're that kid who works with the traveling doctor. I went to a show when he was in town. His older boy, that's the friend you're talking about? He came to the store a while back with the girl who works at the Turners' place. I don't know her last name, only know her as Jennie."

Isaac was here. In Greenville. Right now. "Do you know where I can find her?"

"The Turners live over on Concord Road, just behind the hotel. Look for the house with the painted green door."

Most of the trees that lined Concord were bare, though a few still held to their yellowed leaves. Jack ran down the road, checking doors as he passed. He found the right house close to the end. A girl answered the door. She'd tied a cloth over her hair, her blue eyes just like Isaac's.

"I'm looking for Jennie. Jennie Blum?"

"I'm Jennie." She wasn't much older than Isaac, maybe a year or two more.

"My name is Jack. I work with Dr. Kingsbury. Is Isaac here, by chance?"

"He isn't," Jennie said. "I haven't seen him since the weekend he stayed."

An uneasy feeling grew in Jack's stomach. Where

exactly had Isaac gone? Had he really left on his own, as the doctor had said, or was that another story?

No, Jack thought. Not a story. A lie.

"Is everything all right?" she asked anxiously.

"I'm sorry." Jack didn't want to worry her. "I thought Isaac said he was going to visit. If you see him, could you tell him I stopped by?"

"Yes," Jennie said. "Certainly."

Jack retraced his steps down Concord, the wind scattering leaves at his feet. Maybe the doctor had sent Isaac away and had given him all of the money. Like the pennies the doctor had given Jack, it might have been payment to buy his silence. Or maybe the doctor still had the money and had lied about the theft. And Isaac had left because he was angry, but he hadn't meant to abandon Jack. He'd camped at the saplings and meant to come back once he'd settled down. Only something had happened and he hadn't been able.

Any of those theories could be true. But there was one Jack couldn't escape: Maybe Dr. Kingsbury had something to do with Isaac's disappearance.

He turned from Concord to the main road.

"Any luck?" said the man who'd told Jack about Jennie.

"No. My friend wasn't there."

The man leaned his broom against the wall. "Listen," he said. "I don't know if it's my place to tell you this, but

I figure I will, just the same. That friend of yours, when he was in town, I saw him at the newspaper office. I'd just brought over a delivery. The editor, Stan Grier is his name, he moved here from Indiana a few years back. I overheard him telling your friend that Dr. Kingsbury might have been in some trouble."

"Trouble," Jack said. "What do you mean?"

The man shook his head. "Stan said he wouldn't jump to conclusions. It might only be coincidence. I didn't catch anything else, but your friend was pretty upset. I thought you should know, since you work with him too."

No one answered Jack at the newspaper office. He knocked again, just to be sure.

Isaac had accused the doctor of something, and now he was missing. Gone. Jack tried to breathe, but air refused to fill his chest.

Maybe Isaac hadn't hidden his knapsack. Maybe someone else had stashed it away, hoping it wouldn't be found.

Jack's fingers encircled his tender wrist.

Maybe that someone was Dr. Kingsbury.

AN UNFORTUNATE FALL

"EXCUSE ME, MR. Ogden. Are you all right?"

Walter Ogden had come to town to buy some cheese and bread. He'd been so busy with his Founder's Day history that he hadn't shopped for days. What he hadn't expected were the tonic bottles crammed together in windowsills and toppling onto the road. As he'd passed the graveyard, he swore he'd seen the statue holding one in her hand.

"Mr. Ogden," the person said again.

He shut his eyes to clear his head. "Pardon, what was that?"

In front of Brindley's general store, Cora's mother peered at him. Her brown hair was twisted in intricate ropes and secured at the back of her neck. She wore pearl earrings and a deep blue dress and had a basket of lemons draped over her arm. "I said, is something the matter?"

"Those bottles," he said. "They're everywhere." What had happened at Saturday's medicine show? He hadn't gone to see it. That was the day he'd interviewed a few of Oakdale's older residents. There was no better place to start his history than with the people who knew the town best.

Mrs. Brindley sighed. "Unsightly, isn't it? That doctor's got people believing they can beckon a storm if they buy enough tonic. Who's he to try to challenge the heavens? But that's not what I meant. I didn't see you yesterday."

On Sunday the shaking had been quite bad. He'd stayed home from church to avoid any talk. Today hadn't been much better. Most of it he'd spent behind the safety of his desk. Mr. Ogden crossed his arms and pressed them against his chest. Yet try as he might, he couldn't disguise the movement in his hand.

"Perhaps it's not my concern. I really don't mean to pry." She fiddled with the pearl in her ear. "But when you came through a minute ago, you seemed unsure on your feet."

"I must not have been paying attention," Mr. Ogden said. As he'd stepped from the street onto the sidewalk, his foot had cramped so suddenly, it had been hard for him to move for a moment. If only he weren't so tired and hot.

The bottles weren't the only thing troubling him. He thought he'd known everything about Oakdale, but strange answers had surfaced when he'd asked questions about the tree. The fence he'd always been led to believe was meant as a form of protection. After that fire burned the north part of town two generations ago, the fence was erected to keep the tree safe, to shore up the strength of the town. But that wasn't the story Oakdale's elders had told. Their memories were tinged with fear and doubt. There was more he needed to learn of the story.

He hadn't had as much time as he wanted to think about the history. Because of the hours he'd already given it, he'd stayed up late to finish his lessons. He was tired today, and on days he was weary, the palsy grew stronger. It turned even the smallest effort into a difficult feat.

"The bottles are quite a distraction, aren't they? I'm not sure why the mayor allows them to stay. A mess like this speaks poorly of Oakdale." She rested her hand on the basket of lemons. "What I don't understand is this fascination everyone has with Dr. Kingsbury. I'm glad my Cora hasn't been lured in."

"Cora's a fine girl," Mr. Ogden assured her.

"Thank you." Mrs. Brindley smiled. "I suppose she's getting on well at school?"

"Oh, yes," he said. "Yes, indeed." It wasn't a falsehood. What had happened last week was partly his fault.

There was no need to tell the girls' parents. Cora and Nettie weren't on speaking terms yet, but that day would come. Disagreements couldn't last, not between friends.

"Good. I'm glad to hear it. I'm curious, though, Mr. Ogden. What are your thoughts on Dr. Kingsbury?"

"I don't see any cause for concern." Though after attending a medicine show and meeting the doctor in the grove, there was little he knew of the man.

"No one can say where the doctor came from. And that tonic of his—who has any idea what's in it? You know I support the temperance movement. We encourage self-restraint, the practice of moderation. There are some who have no control in the presence of strong drink. Don't you remember, Mr. Ogden, how the Ladies' Auxiliary marched last spring and demanded the tavern be closed?"

"Well, yes," he said, uncertain where this conversation was going.

"And now," Mrs. Brindley continued, "after all our good efforts, here's a stranger selling tonic from the back of a wagon. How can we be certain that his medicine isn't alcohol?"

"I can't imagine it is," Mr. Ogden said. He'd taken the tonic for over a week. While the medicine had a powerful flavor, he hadn't tasted any spirits.

The sun beat down mercilessly. He wiped his face with a handkerchief. It was hotter than any October in memory.

If he wanted to get his shopping done, he'd have to attend to it now. "It's good to see you, Mrs. Brindley, but I must get on with my—"

"Pardon me." Worry marked the woman's face. "But is something wrong with your fingers?"

He squeezed his hand into a fist, crumpling the handkerchief. "It's nothing." This was why he'd kept to himself. Why he'd avoided church and coming to town.

"I could get you some help. Let me call Mr. Brindley."

"No. There's no need for that. I promise you, I'm perfectly fine." He didn't need a school board trustee asking after his health.

Mr. Ogden reached for the door, making sure to use his steady hand. This time when he stumbled, he fell. There were no bottles he could blame.

A MISSING BAG

JACK HURRIED THROUGH the knee-high grass. Overhead, clouds towered and climbed. He had only a few minutes to himself. He had to find Isaac's bag again.

Since yesterday's visit to Greenville, Jack had gone over it all in his head. Isaac had learned something about Dr. Kingsbury, and now Isaac was gone. The doctor might be in some sort of trouble, the man at the grocery said. That must have been what set Isaac off, what made him confront the doctor. Jack pushed aside brambles and prickly grass, hurrying as fast as he could.

All morning, Jack had watched Dr. Kingsbury to see if his behavior had changed, but the doctor acted the same as before. With each customer, he listened attentively. He was patient, never hurrying anyone, but giving each person the time they needed. Of course, there was no reason for his behavior to change since yesterday. It was Jack's thoughts that had shifted when he'd heard the grocer's story.

He was certain now Dr. Kingsbury was involved in Isaac's disappearance.

He slowed as he neared the sapling grove not far from the riverbank. Maybe there was something in the bag that he'd missed, a clue that might tell him what Isaac had learned. Jack pushed through the trees until he reached an opening in the underbrush. He got on his knees and felt for the bag. Nothing was there. Jack moved to a new spot and tried again.

The bag was gone. Someone had taken it.

He grabbed a small branch and snapped it in half. Jack kicked a pile of leaves. Then he stilled because of a terrible thought.

What if the doctor had taken the bag so no one else would find it?

THE PLAY'S THE THING

COME BACK TOMORROW. The sign leaned against the wagon, its words painted in red and brown. Jack started up the wagon steps. "Cora, follow me."

Since yesterday, Isaac's missing bag had been all Jack could think about. Earlier, when the doctor left to talk with the mayor about Founder's Day, Jack had run to the graveyard to leave a note, asking Cora to meet him in the grove.

A strip of sun spilled across the floor. Light seeped through the wagon's high window. It wasn't much for them to see by, but he wouldn't light the candles again.

"Jack?" Cora said. "What are we doing?"

"We're going to look for Isaac's bag."

He'd told her everything when she'd gotten there. His

suspicions about the tonic. The lies about it bringing the rain. At Saturday's show, the doctor had claimed that last Monday a man had told him a story. The man swore the tonic had awakened the winds and made the clouds form. All that day Jack had worked beside the doctor, collecting coins and handing out tonic. Not once had a man said anything like that. "If someone told that story, it was Dr. Kingsbury. He must have whispered it to a customer while I fetched some of the tonic."

"I heard talk that same day that it might bring the rain. But why would the doctor do that?"

Jack shrugged. "To sell more bottles. To bring more customers to the grove. Whatever he says, I can't believe him. The doctor is a fraud." The word was ugly, like a bone stripped of its flesh. For days it had run through Jack's mind. He'd practiced it under his breath.

He'd told her about Isaac, too. How Isaac was his friend who'd worked for the doctor. How he'd disappeared after an argument, and Dr. Kingsbury had accused him of stealing his money. How last week Jack had found Isaac's bag, but yesterday it was gone.

Cora looked in the dark space under the desk. "Do you think the doctor has hidden it somewhere?"

"That's what I want to find out."

Jack opened a dusty trunk but only discovered blankets and rags. Cora found nothing in the cupboards or crates.

Then Jack thought of the drawer he was never to touch. The bag was too big to fit inside, but the doctor could have stashed something in it.

Jack smoothed his palm along the desk until he found the handle. He pulled, but the drawer didn't budge. "The key," he said. "I'm not sure where he keeps it."

Cora checked in the jars of herbs and the mortar's hollowed cup. Jack felt underneath the bookcase. They couldn't find it anywhere.

He tugged the handle one more time. "We need some other way to get it open."

"Your pocketknife," Cora said. "Could I borrow it?"

He took out his blade and gave it to her.

"My cousin Cuthbert did this once." She pushed the tip of the knife in the keyhole. Jack heard a faint click as she twisted the blade. She pulled, and the drawer only opened halfway, but wide enough for him to reach in his hand.

Sweat trickled down his face. He wiped it with his sleeve. "The only thing here is the bag of coins."

Maybe the money was all there was, but Jack couldn't leave without being certain. He gripped the handle and yanked again. The wooden drawer slipped free from the desk. Jack checked every corner, but apart from the pouch, the drawer was empty.

Why had he expected anything different?

But when he pushed the drawer back into place, Jack heard a crinkling sound.

"Did you hear that?" Cora said. "Inch the drawer forward, slowly this time."

There it was again, like the crush of dry leaves.

"I bet something's stuck in the back."

Jack pulled out the drawer a second time and stretched his arm into the empty space. Paper was wedged in the top of the desk. He wiggled it loose and pushed the drawer back. "Let's go," he said. "Down to the river."

The two of them ran. They settled behind the slab of rock, a place they'd stay unseen. Jack unfolded the paper carefully.

"It's a newspaper clipping," Cora said.

Above the story was a sketch of a man in old-fashioned pantaloons. The sleeves of his shirt gathered in pleats. A cape reached the backs of his knees. In his hand, the man held a human skull.

His face was unmistakable.

Cora gasped. "It's Dr. Kingsbury!"

"Here," Jack said. "I'll read it."

THE PLAY'S THE THING:
A Rousing Portrayal of Hamlet

WABASH—City Park is hosting Dun's Theatrical Troupe

for the summer of '81. In the past four weeks, the troupe has staged four different Shakespearean plays, a new one every week. Last night's *Hamlet* far exceeded the others. The principal player, Elijah Barry, is the primary reason. He performs the role of the Danish prince with depth and emotional truth.

One might consider Barry's towering physical presence at odds with the sensitivity an actor must bring to the role, yet Barry convincingly portrays the conflicted young man. From Hamlet's early encounter with his father's ghost, to his conversation with Yorick's skull, to the final act and his tragic end, Barry's performance is sure to win any audience over.

"The stage," Barry says, "is where I feel most at home." Welcome home, Elijah Barry. Wabash is grateful you're here.

Alan Egan plays the role of Claudius. Beatrice Clark plays Gertrude. *Hamlet* runs through Saturday evening. Be sure not to miss this outstanding cultural event.

The doctor had been an actor onstage. It was written right there in the newspaper.

"Kingsbury's not his name," Cora said.

A nettlesome feeling pricked Jack's chest. He scrambled to the riverbed. Jack dipped his hands in the water and washed them over his face. Cold ran down his neck. His shirt clung to his skin.

Cora picked up the paper where Jack had dropped it and met him at the river. "Didn't Dr. Kingsbury say he'd sold tonic for twelve years? But this story's from 1881. That was only six years ago."

The river raced over the stones. It turned and tumbled as it always did, as though nothing had changed when everything had—who the doctor was, what he'd really been doing those years he'd claimed he'd been on the road.

"I think the doctor hurt Isaac—or worse." Jack couldn't bring himself to say the word that lurked on the edge of his thoughts. Small hints had surfaced that he'd tried to ignore. When he'd returned the shirt in the strange silence, like no one but Jack had been there for days. When Jennie Blum hadn't seen Isaac. When his bag had disappeared.

"Isaac discovered something the doctor didn't want him to know." Jack's stomach clenched. "Maybe it was something like this."

What if he went missing? How long would it take for his family to find out? Would anyone else notice or care?

Cora touched his wrist, where the bruise had yellowed. "Did the doctor do this to you?"

"Jack?" Dr. Kingsbury called. "Jack? Are you there?" There was the sound of footsteps coming closer. "Where's that boy gone now?"

Jack took the paper from Cora and tucked it in his sleeve. He signaled for her to stay where she was. "Here I am," he said as he left the river.

The drawer was still unlocked. If Dr. Kingsbury checked, he'd find the story missing.

AN INVITATION RECONSIDERED

MISS MOORE LOOKED up from the bonnet she was stitching as someone opened the door.

"My goodness," she heard a woman say. "What a strange place Oakdale's become, with all those bottles about. I'm not sure what your father's thinking."

She knew that voice. It was Alma James, probably coming to pick up her hat. Was it already Tuesday? Miss Moore checked her ledger. The days had gotten away from her. As for Oakdale, she'd always found the town peculiar. The parades, the nonsense in the park, the regular festivities. Those rules about the oak—do not climb, do not even touch. What child didn't long to do both? The tree was magnificent, she had to agree, but that was no reason to set it apart.

After the last medicine show, a frenzy had erupted in town. Since Saturday, four people had asked if they could put tonic in her windows—as if she'd consent to such a thing.

Miss Moore set down the bonnet and walked to the front of the shop. "Good afternoon," she said to Mrs. James. The woman was with her daughter, a girl who must have been about twelve and was almost as tall as her mother. A yellow braid hung down the girl's back. Her chin was marked with a few red spots, no more than was typical for someone her age. Whether Kingsbury's tonic had helped her complexion was not for Miss Moore to say.

"Hello," Mrs. James said. A few loose tendrils of hair framed her delicate face. "I'm here to pick up my hat." Her cheeks pinkened a little. "The order for Alma James."

Perhaps it had been unkind, pretending last time to forget her name. "Yes, Mrs. James. I remember. Give me a moment, please."

"Look at this! It's beautiful!"

As she fetched the hat from the back of the shop, Miss Moore could hear the girl gush. Most likely she'd seen the unfinished bonnet. The pale green ribbon stitched to the brim would complement the girl's coloring.

Miss Moore set a box on the countertop and lifted the hat from its wrappings.

"How lovely!" Alma stroked the gray felt. "You've outdone yourself again."

A faint smile appeared on Miss Moore's lips. She'd never wear felt in this heat. And while she wouldn't have paired a red rose with the gray, she had to admit it was excellent work. It pleased her when others took notice. "Try it on. See how it looks. I'll go fetch the mirror."

Mrs. James turned her head this way and that, admiring her reflection.

The girl nudged her mother's arm. "Ask about the other one. Please?"

"The bonnet you're working on," Mrs. James said. "Is it meant for anyone in particular?"

"It isn't. Your daughter may try it on if she likes."

Carefully, the girl tied the ribbons. She grinned at herself in the mirror.

"It's perfect. Just right for the tea." Mrs. James reached for her purse. "We'll take them both, Miss Moore."

Two sales in the span of a minute. The day was coming together quite nicely.

In the last weeks, business had slowed. The money usually spent in the shops was probably going to him. The showman. That's how Miss Moore thought of Kingsbury now. Most likely the name was a pseudonym. She wasn't about to call the man *doctor*, even though his tonic had brought her relief.

Miss Moore drew her needle from the hat's brim. "Let me just finish stitching the ribbon."

The girl wandered the shop as she waited. She was old enough to keep her hands to herself, which Miss Moore was grateful for. Her mother hovered near the counter. "I hope," she said, "you might consider attending the Auxiliary Tea."

Miss Moore tugged her needle, pulling until the thread was taut.

"I'd be much obliged if you joined us."

At home in Indiana, neighbors gathered for special occasions. But here the women of Oakdale met together incessantly. Didn't they see enough of each other at the church, in the shops, at the town's celebrations?

"I don't know about that," Miss Moore said. "My work keeps me quite busy."

"Even so, we'd be happy for you to come. Your aunt Matilda was a favorite of my mother, Evangeline Cook."

Miss Moore remembered the thoughtful gift when Aunt Matilda died. One morning, not long after the funeral, she'd found a box on the steps of her shop. Inside was a beautiful shawl. *Your aunt made this for my mother. I thought you might enjoy it now.* The note was signed *Alma James.*

"It will be my mother's sixty-sixth birthday. I hope you might consider it. A body needs companionship, and sometimes I worry . . ." Alma James dropped her gaze and fidgeted with her sleeve.

She worried Miss Moore didn't have any friends in this

town where outsiders didn't fit in. Whether that was true or not was none of this woman's business. Usually, such a remark would draw a sharp word from Eloise Moore. But not today. Maybe it was because she'd sold two hats. Or the three days she'd had with no trace of a headache since she'd started mixing some tonic in with her morning tea.

"I'll come," she said, surprising herself.

"That's wonderful! It's Thursday at three o'clock. You needn't bring a thing." Alma scribbled her address on a piece of paper.

Miss Moore knotted her thread and cut off the end. She had committed herself. There was no going back. "Very well," she said. "I'll see you then."

A DECISION REACHED

WALTER OGDEN SAT on his bed in the darkness, holding his head in his hands. At dusk, he'd lighted the lamp on his nightstand. How long ago had that been?

It was Wednesday night. Twelve days of tonic had made no difference. At first he'd been hopeful, especially the morning when the tremors had started later than usual, but the following day, the shaking had been more pronounced than before.

He no longer believed the tonic would help him. His body was broken, with the palsy to blame. There was no use pretending otherwise.

There was no chance he'd marry. No woman would ever want him like this. He'd never grow old with someone he loved or have children of his own. One idea circled and circled his mind, the most painful thought of all. If the palsy was his burden to carry, it wouldn't be long before he lost his job teaching.

When he'd fallen at the general store, Mr. Brindley had been more than kind to him. The man had helped him to a chair and had given him a cupful of water. Walter was certain Mr. Brindley had seen the tremor in his hand. He'd tried to hold his body still, but sitting there, out in the open, there'd been nowhere to hide the trembling. Mr. Brindley never said a word, but he'd seen the concern in the man's sideways glances. Mr. Ogden had imagined the Brindleys discussing his health together that night. He'd wondered if later Mr. Brindley had talked to the rest of the school board trustees.

His fingers pulsed as he gripped his hair. He'd never escape the trembling. The more he wished for the tremor to stop, the fiercer the palsy became.

At first, when his symptoms hadn't abated, he'd thought the tonic needed more time. He'd been so busy recently. He was almost done with the history paper that he'd written for Founder's Day. His focus was the fire of 1836 and the fencing of the tree. It was nothing like what he'd learned in school or the history that he'd taught his own students. But the piece had started to come together once he'd talked to

Evangeline Cook. After probing a few others who'd been alive then, he was confident in what he'd written.

There was only one interview left. Tomorrow evening with Henry Graham. It had been difficult to secure an appointment after the second medicine show. Since his healing, Mr. Graham had been swamped with invitations and uninvited guests, but at last, he'd agreed.

The school board wouldn't expect this paper, but in this year of the drought and the palsy and the doctor, Walter Ogden had learned not to be shocked by anything.

What he had to accept was the thought that had come in his hours of sitting alone. As he'd stilled his mind, the thought had grown more clear and distinct: His teaching this term was an empty husk, a dried-up pod with its center missing. Compared to his efforts in other years, he'd done little to help his students.

They deserved so much more than he could offer.

Mr. Ogden stood. He moved through the gloom to the lamp's gleaming light and extinguished the wavering flame. He'd go to Mr. Brindley. He'd ask him to gather the school board together to meet at the end of the week. On Friday, at the end of the day.

He would tell them together—the trustees and his students. He wouldn't just tell them, he'd show how the tremor overpowered his hand. Once they'd seen, he'd do the board a favor and offer his resignation. His parents could take him in for a time until he could find another job—if there was anyone willing to hire him. Or maybe he could go to his sister's family and find work in another town.

The pressure in his shoulders eased. He was tired of hiding, so worn down from hoping. Friday would be the worst day of his life.

It would come as a welcome relief.

THE AUXILIARY TEA

AUNT ALMA SMILED as she opened the gate. She kissed Cora's cheek. "Welcome to your first Auxiliary Tea."

Cora hadn't counted down to the tea, not like Nettie had been doing for weeks. But she had been looking forward to Nana's birthday. How wonderful to turn a regular Thursday into a celebration!

"Where are Mother and Lauren?" Aunt Alma asked.

"They're running behind, but they're coming soon."

The garden, usually a commotion of color, had faded in the autumn heat. The impatiens had wilted, the roses had browned, the vines were no longer a vibrant green. The tree in the center of the garden burned in shades of yellow and red. Six tables encircled its thickened trunk. Nettie moved from table to table, laying the silverware. She wore a new bonnet with a green satin ribbon.

Cora tugged the brim of her hat—an old one of Mother's from two summers ago. She'd thought it was stylish at first, but seeing Nettie's fashionable bonnet made her realize that hers was out of date.

"I've brought lemon tea cakes," Cora said. She tried to pretend everything was fine. They didn't need to argue, not on Nana's special day.

"Put them here." Nettie thumped the tea cart with her hand. She didn't look up from the work she was doing. "Where's everyone else?"

Mother and Nana hadn't been ready when Cora got home from school. Something had been bothering Nana. She was searching through her room and the kitchen shelves. Cora asked if she needed any help, but Nana said she couldn't remember. "Go on without us," Mother said. Cora had left with the basket of cakes.

"They'll be here soon," she told Nettie.

She wandered the tables reading the name cards, looking for Brindley and James and Cook. She found them at a table with a seat for Miss Moore. Gently she touched her grandmother's card. Hopefully Nana's mind had settled by now.

"What are you doing?" Nettie asked.

Cora didn't have to say. She pulled out her chair next to the one that had been set aside for Nettie.

Voices drifted from the gate. Mrs. Wells rounded the corner, followed by Mrs. Kennedy. Why were Mother and Nana taking so long? The garden filled with Auxiliary members, their bonnets as bright as flower bouquets.

"Welcome," Aunt Alma said. "Everyone, please find your seats. I'm so glad you've come to the Auxiliary Tea."

There Mother and Nana were. Nana was draped in her white tasseled shawl. Quietly, Mother shut the gate.

"It's hot," Aunt Alma went on, "but the breeze should keep us comfortable. Be sure to drink some lemonade."

"Sorry we're late," Mother said when she and Nana got to the table.

"Happy birthday." Nettie kissed her grandmother's cheek.

Nana watched the sky overhead. The gauze of her bonnet matched the hastening clouds.

"We'll start at half past the hour," Aunt Alma said. "Millie will bring the tea cart by. Make the most of this lovely afternoon!" She came to the table and kissed her mother. "I hope this day is perfect for you."

"Thank you, my dear. Everything's lovely."

Nettie perched on the side of her chair near Miss Moore's empty spot, as far from Cora as she could get.

"Alma," Mother said, "I've been meaning to ask. Why has Nathanael let Dr. Kingsbury make such a mess of our town?"

Aunt Alma looked a little embarrassed. "Those bottles are rather awful, I know, but the tonic has done so much good for Nathanael. He's able to sleep now that he's taking it."

Mother drew a sharp breath. "What is Nathanael thinking? No one knows who that man is or what's in his tonic."

"You could ask Cora." Nettie smiled, pleased with herself. "She's friends with the doctor's boy."

Cora smacked Nettie's leg under the table. How dare Nettie try to get her in trouble! First Nettie had threatened to tell on her and then she'd stolen her journal. Why couldn't Nettie leave her alone? It was all tied to Jack somehow. Nettie didn't like that she'd found a new friend. Well, too bad. That wasn't changing. Cora picked up her chair and turned it around so her back was facing Nettie.

A frigid tone came to Mother's voice. "The doctor's boy? Cora, is that true?"

Cora studied the napkin she'd spread in her lap. If only Miss Moore would hurry. She would move the conversation in another direction, like the newest ways to trim a bonnet, or how people in Indiana passed these hot autumn days.

"I don't want you involved with that doctor."

"Hush now, Lauren," Nana said. "I think it's nice Cora's made a friend."

Never had Cora been so grateful for Millie as when she appeared with the cart. Millie heaped Nettie's plate with cucumber sandwiches. She filled Cora's glass with lemonade. Nana nibbled on a raspberry scone. For a moment everything else was forgotten.

Conversation drifted from nearby—the number of eggs in a Kennedy pound cake. The new words the Mueller baby could speak. The costumes planned for Founder's Day. And the tonic, always the tonic: Who used it. Who should try a dose. The number of bottles in Ada Brown's window—had anyone counted how many?

Nana set down her raspberry scone. "Where's Silas? I hoped to see him today."

"Silas," Mother said. "Who's he?"

Cora looked into her grandmother's eyes. "Nana, you know Silas?"

"Of course I do. He's my oldest friend."

Cora remembered the girl and the fire. The story of the boy and the drought. "Is he the one? The boy you said who got the blame?"

"No one believed me," Nana said. "I was only a child."

It was too strange to consider that Nana knew Silas, too strange and perfectly fitting, that the kind old man Cora had befriended was once Nana's friend, too.

But why had he come back after all these years?

A breeze rustled the tablecloth. Cora grabbed her napkin as it fell from her lap. Above the tree, darkening clouds raced to cover the sun.

The wind gusted and carried with it a flurry of conversation.

"Maybe the rain's finally . . ."

"Please! Help me chase down my hat!"

". . . storm by tonight at the latest."

"Goodness." Aunt Alma stood so quickly, she bumped the table with her knee. "This weather isn't cooperating. We best move inside."

Without further instruction, Millie pushed the cart to the door.

"Gather your dishes!" Aunt Alma called. "We will continue in the parlor."

Nana reached for Mother's arm, white tassels fluttering like leaves.

Cora tucked her glass in the crook of her elbow and clutched her plate with both hands. She followed Nettie, taking short, measured steps. Inside, the smell of furniture wax mingled with Uncle's tobacco smoke. A portrait of Robert Frasier hung over the mantelpiece. Nettie was certain he'd had a sweet tooth. She could tell, she'd once said, by the shape of his chin.

The Ladies' Auxiliary settled in as comfortably as they could. Some sat on the sofa or the spindle-backed chairs.

Others stood with their plates in their hands. Cora sat down on the rug next to Nettie, only because there was nowhere else to go. They were so close, their knees almost touched. It was enough to make Cora scoot over to open a space between them.

Aunt Alma continued as if nothing had changed. "If you haven't gotten your tea yet, Millie will be by shortly. Mrs. Wells, are you ready to begin?"

Mrs. Wells came to the front of the room, right under the portrait of Uncle Robert. The two of them shared the same rounded chin. He looked weary up there, Cora thought, tired of hanging on the wall.

"Thank you, Alma," Mrs. Wells said, "for hosting us today. This year marks the hundred and tenth anniversary of the founding of our organization. When I was elected president last spring . . ." She spoke on about meetings and members.

Outside, the wind moaned. There were whispers of rain, but when Cora watched through the window, she didn't see anything.

Mrs. Wells talked on about rules and future calendar dates. Cora peeked at Nettie, who nibbled a sandwich. She wasn't beholden to Nettie's demands. She could choose any friend she liked.

". . . will honor Evangeline Cook on her birthday. Evangeline, could you please come forward?"

Cora set her plate aside, intent on listening. Slowly, Nana moved to the front. How dear she looked in her white bonnet. It was a perfect match for her shawl. Her eyes were sharp and inquisitive as she took a seat in a wingback chair next to the fireplace. Whatever had muddled her earlier, it seemed like it had passed.

"When a child is born," Mrs. Wells went on, "when a family loses a loved one to death, and during illness or celebration, we as an Auxiliary care for our town. For years, Evangeline Cook has served our community. On behalf of the Auxiliary, we thank you, Evangeline, for your tireless work."

"It's been my pleasure."

"We wish you the happiest of birthdays. Is there anything you'd like to say?"

Nana looked at the room of familiar faces. "I love this town. It's my life's joy working alongside all of you. Oakdale has a proud history of caring for its own." Nana lifted her eyes to Mrs. Wells. "But perhaps we're too proud at times."

"Too proud?" Mrs. Wells faltered. "I don't quite understand."

"Maybe we're too quick to defend. Like the night Henry Graham set the barn on fire."

"Henry Graham set a fire?" someone said.

Cora heard a rattle at the latch. At first she thought it

was the wind. Then the handle turned, and the door pushed open. Silently, Miss Moore slipped in. Her dress was filthy. Hair tumbled down her back.

"Long ago," Nana answered. "I saw Henry running across McCalls' field. I told everyone he'd set the fire, but no one believed what I said."

A LETTER FROM HOME

ELOISE MOORE WAS late to the tea because the wind had taken her hat. As she'd stepped to the sidewalk in front of her shop, a gust of air had lifted it. The hat had sailed beyond her hands, skimming the road like a twig in a stream.

She wasn't going to lose her best bonnet, a hat of cornflower blue. It was newly made with an ostrich plume pinned smartly on the back. Miss Moore had grabbed her skirts, ready to chase the bonnet down, when she snagged her boot on the edge of the sidewalk. Along with a jumble of tonic bottles, she toppled into the street.

Caught in a current near Brindley's store, her hat skipped farther on. It sailed beyond the steps of the bank, passing under the banner for Founder's Day. As it neared the square, a blast of air carried it even higher.

She watched, transfixed, from where she'd fallen. Had she tripped or was it a dizzy spell? She'd been feeling unsteady since yesterday.

The hat sailed high above and stuck in the old oak tree. Ribbons tangled around its limbs. The ostrich plume bobbed in the breeze. The hat was too high to poke with a broom, if such a thing were allowed in this town with its tree and its rules and its dastardly heat.

"Do you need any help?"

She looked over her shoulder. The doctor's boy. He'd probably seen everything.

"I don't," she said curtly. Miss Moore dusted her skirts. "It's you who need to take care with the doctor."

If only she'd left that letter from home until after she'd gone to the tea.

The wind had been calm when she'd heard the mail drop. A letter from home, when she hadn't had any for weeks. Every note from Mother started the same. She was hardy and hale with no twinge of illness, though last summer had been a trial. Her pansies hadn't been as fragrant as usual, her geraniums had withered and died—both due to the sweltering heat.

The second part of Mother's letter had been quite a shock:

What a surprise, Mother had written, *that you asked about the McPherson boy.* There was a recent story about him in the Wabash Weekly. *Years ago, you might remember, his mother had gone through his things. She'd found a list of numbers alongside a name. Barry, that was the name he'd written down. It seemed Ernest had gotten in gambling trouble with the likes of that theatrical troupe, and the list was of money he owed. Remember? He'd worked as a stagehand the summer we saw those plays in the park.*

A watch was recently found in the river, the inside monogrammed with his initials. The McPhersons say the watch was his, but Ernest had never learned to swim. The police now suspect he came to some harm. Would you believe, they think that actor, the one who played Hamlet, was somehow involved. Him! The tall one with the thick mane of hair. It was his name on Ernest's list.

Can you even imagine?

It took months for police to find the troupe. The man had left them years ago. He'd given up acting, the others said, not long after their summer here.

The McPhersons are getting on all right, but I don't know what to think. Why would a man with such talent leave the stage unless he had something to hide?

"Take care with the doctor?" the boy said.

She could have been kinder to the child. He wasn't to blame for the doctor's work. But she wasn't feeling entirely right. She was late, and the wind had stolen her hat.

Because she'd taken her time leaving the shop.

Because she'd read the letter from home.

"What's your name?" she asked the child.

He dipped his chin. "It's Jack."

"Well, Jack, I'm Miss Moore, and I happen to know a boy's gone missing. Ask your Dr. Kingsbury about it."

Jack pushed the hair out of his eyes. They were eyes that carried pain. "You know about Isaac?"

"Isaac?" she said. "Who's that? I'm talking about a boy from my town. His name was Ernest McPherson."

BEFORE A TOWN TURNS

CLOUDS CLIMBED THE darkening sky, their bellies swollen with rain. Jack left the road from Oakdale and took the path to the grove. He wished he could forget what Miss Moore had said. Ernest McPherson had been her classmate in Indiana when she was a girl. He'd gone missing years ago. The doctor might be to blame. This had to be what Isaac had learned, what the newspaper man had told him about.

Jack passed under the willow trees. When he reached the clearing, no one was there. An hour ago, when the doctor had sent him on a quick errand, dozens of customers had waited in line. Now the sign was propped against the wagon. Had the doctor sold out of tonic that quickly?

"Dr. Kingsbury?"

No one answered.

The doctor hadn't mentioned meeting the mayor. Or maybe he had, and Jack didn't remember. Since Jack and Cora had found the newspaper clipping, it had been hard for him to think of much else. The play called *Hamlet*. The actor named Barry. The drawing of Dr. Kingsbury.

If the doctor was gone, Jack could return it.

The steps creaked under his feet. He opened the heavy door. It took a moment for his eyes to adjust to the wagon's dim interior.

"I've been waiting for you." Dr. Kingsbury sat behind his desk. Sputtering candles cast shadows on the angles of his face.

Dread surged in Jack's middle. The walls pressed close enough to suffocate.

"I knew you couldn't resist coming in. Bet you're here to put back the article, aren't you?" Dr. Kingsbury held out his hand. "Give it to me."

The newspaper clipping was damp in Jack's fingers as he placed it in the doctor's palm.

"Perhaps it was foolish of me to keep, but I've always been fond of the story. What does it say? 'Kingsbury's performance will win any audience over'?"

"Not Kingsbury," Jack said, before he could think. "The newspaper called you Barry."

It was the same name Miss Moore had used. Sweat

trickled between Jack's shoulder blades. Everything he knew of the doctor was wrong. It was all a performance, a well-rehearsed play.

"Barry, yes. It's been a long time since I've heard that name. But we have other things to discuss." The doctor leaned close. "The day after tomorrow is Founder's Day. The rains must come soon, or people will doubt. Remember this, Jack. It's best to leave before a town turns."

"Before it turns?"

Candlelight shone in the doctor's eyes. "Before it turns to hostility. It's best to go before anger sets in, while people still have faith."

A gust of wind battered the window. The heat stayed close, oppressive and thick. Jack reached for the desk to steady himself. "Why are you telling me this?"

"It's time you understood some things." Dr. Kingsbury unfolded the paper and spread it flat. "Those were good years, the ones on the stage. When a man has a talent like mine, it doesn't quite work to be part of a troupe. At some point, he must break free."

The doctor left his stool and settled himself on the edge of the desk. "Twelve years I've spent on the road, not all of them as Kingsbury. I was lucky to meet Kilmer when I did. He was ready to be done with doctoring. I needed a new trade. He sold me his wagon and his recipe, too. It's not too different from my theater days. I bring my audience what they need. A break from the ordinary. A measure of faith. A diversion to offset life's drudgeries. And help in the form of my tonic.

"You're a sensible boy, not like that Isaac," Dr. Kingsbury said. "Surely you've realized by now that the tonic can't cure every last ailment. But really, what medicine could? I can offer hope, but there are no guarantees. Ginger soothes unsettled stomachs. Snakeroot eases pain. A rinse with tonic clears an ear of its wax. The rest?" He shrugged. "Who's to say? If someone feels better after taking it, what's so wrong with that?" The doctor lifted a half-empty bottle, the one that once held the poppies he'd worn in his buttonhole. "You can't forget how the tonic helped Lucy."

Jack nodded, tears burning his eyes. Because he'd seen something next to the bottle. A wooden rabbit full of life, crouched as though it were ready to spring. He dug his fingernails into his palms. He needed the pain, its sharpened edges.

"It's quite good, isn't it?" Dr. Kingsbury said when he saw what had drawn Jack's attention. "I always admired Isaac's craftsmanship. It's too bad what had to happen to him."

"What happened?" Jack whispered.

The doctor's dark eyes lingered on him. "He overstepped. He chose his fate. It's sad, really, when you think of it. Isaac was an accomplished young man. We could have worked together for years. I hoped to train him to take over someday and run the show on his own."

Dr. Kingsbury had killed Isaac. He'd told Jack as much without saying the words. But why had he stayed in the town where it happened? Why hadn't he left immediately?

"But what about . . ." Jack wasn't sure quite how to ask. "What about Isaac's family?"

"The boy had little family to speak of. There's no one to miss him but that penniless maid."

"Did he really steal your money?" Jack said before he could stop himself.

The doctor waved the question away. "A ploy to keep you from the drawer, though I see it wasn't enough to sway you." The doctor grabbed Jack's arm, fingers digging into flesh. "Listen. Don't forget your place. Don't think of behaving as Isaac did. You have nowhere to go. No money to speak of. If you tried to tell someone, who would believe you?"

Cora, Jack thought. Cora would.

There was a scratch at the wagon's door. Bear whined from the other side.

The doctor tightened his grip. "Think how lonely that dog would be if something happened to you."

Dr. Kingsbury yanked Jack close enough that he could feel the doctor's breath on his cheek.

The pain was so bad Jack could barely stand.

"Watch yourself. I mean it."

A BITTER LESSON

THE SCHOOL DAY was almost over when Mr. Ogden greeted the men at the door. They shut out the rest of the room in their tight circle of shoulders and backs. Behind her, Cora could hear the boys whispering. She peeked at Nettie, who looked up in surprise. Briefly, their eyes met.

Why was the school board here? Sometimes Father or Mr. Mueller stopped by, but never the whole board at once.

Cora closed her lesson book, not bothering to mark her place.

The circle of men broke apart. Father clasped Mr. Ogden's shoulder and whispered. Mr. Ogden nodded and turned to the class. "You may set your lessons aside."

Exhilaration traveled the room. The school board

retreated to the back. Father brushed Cora's arm as he walked by, light enough that she thought he might not have meant it. Mr. Ogden perched on the edge of his desk, his arms crossed over his middle.

Tears pricked Cora's eyes, though she wasn't sure why.

"I have something to show all of you." He uncrossed his arms and lifted one hand. His fingers fumbled and twitched. "Can everyone see? If you need to move closer, come sit in the front."

Cuthbert and Benjamin left their seats. Janie Kennedy slipped from her desk and knelt on the floor.

"I'm not trying to move my hand. It's doing this on its own."

This felt like a lesson, a demonstration to help with their learning, like the counting beans Mr. Ogden kept in a jar on his desk. Cora squeezed her hands into fists, pressing so hard her fingers ached. Because this was bigger than a school lesson. She didn't want to hear any more.

"The shaking started early this term. It's gotten worse as the weeks have passed. Sometimes my foot seizes up, making it hard to move."

Cora remembered watching from Nana's window, how Mr. Ogden had struggled to walk.

"I haven't been myself," he said. "I wanted to tell you I'm sorry for that."

"What's happened?" Cuthbert asked.

"I think it's the shaking palsy."

Cuthbert dug in his pocket and pulled out a bottle. "You could try the tonic. It fixed up my toe."

Mr. Ogden crouched down beside Cuthbert and looked into his eyes. "I've tried the tonic for almost two weeks. Nothing is different. I don't think it will change."

"Excuse me," Mr. Mueller said from the back, "but I don't know how that's possible. Palsy's an illness of a much older man. Don't you remember Joe McCall?"

Mr. McCall had shuffled along, barely lifting his feet. Sometimes he'd stopped altogether, as though he'd forgotten where he needed to be or as if his legs could no longer take him. The twitch in his fingers and his garbled speech had frightened Cora when she was small.

Would the same happen to Mr. Ogden?

"I know it's unusual," Mr. Ogden said, "but I've talked to the doctor, and he agrees." He struggled a little as he tried to stand. "This is the school where I grew up. I wanted to teach here for the rest of my life. I'm sorry for not being the teacher you need."

"Cora," someone whispered nearby.

Nettie stood in the aisle; her face had gone white. She slipped in next to Cora and reached for her hand. Nettie's fingers were sweaty and warm. Cora didn't push her away, but she didn't return Nettie's squeeze, either. She knew Nettie was worried, too, but that didn't fix what had happened between them.

"The last teacher was asked to leave when an illness he had became chronic. I want to make it easier this time. This is my last term at Oakdale School. I'm resigning as your teacher."

A rumble of voices arose. Cora jumped to her feet. "No. Please don't go!" What did it matter if his hands shook? That didn't change who Mr. Ogden was—the best teacher she'd ever had.

Cuthbert shouted, "We want you to stay!"

Janie Kennedy leaped from the floor and wrapped her arms around their teacher.

The school board huddled in the back of the room, deep in conversation.

"Please, Mr. Ogden," Cora said. "Please. Promise you'll reconsider."

FINISHED

JACK WOKE TO lightning that burned the sky. He wasn't certain he'd really slept. Yesterday had been hard, but the night was worse. In the dark his thoughts wouldn't leave him alone.

The doctor had ended Isaac's life. He'd possibly done the same to Ernest.

Jack was indebted to Dr. Kingsbury. He'd thought the tonic had saved his sister. But the medicine wasn't a miracle cure. His time with the doctor had been a lie.

Though for days, the clouds had gathered and grown, there still hadn't been any rain. The sky flashed again and the thunder answered, a rolling that echoed inside Jack's chest. He pushed off his blanket and reached for his shoes. Bear followed him to the river, his shadow on the darkened path.

He couldn't stop thinking about Jennie Blum. She needed to hear what had happened to Isaac. But how could Jack tell her what he didn't know? When he'd been in Greenville, he hadn't said anything. That omission had been a lie.

There'd been other falsehoods, too. Some Jack hadn't realized were lies when he'd told them, though that didn't make them any less wrong. Oakdale believed the doctor worked miracles partly because of Jack and his story. At the second show he could have told the truth, but instead he'd kept to the lie.

A jagged bolt slashed the dark. Its light gleamed in the curve of the river. Jack felt for the pennies the doctor had given him. Five coins, like any others, with only one small difference. These bound him to Dr. Kingsbury. These pennies had paid for his silence. He'd betrayed Isaac in saving them and misled Oakdale, too.

For almost two weeks, they'd weighed him down. He could rid himself of their burden now.

Jack threw the first penny as hard as he could. It sailed through the air and disappeared in the river. He threw the next and the next until every penny was gone.

He was done with the doctor. He needed to go, but not

before Founder's Day. He owed it to Isaac and Ernest and Oakdale. Tomorrow, he'd tell the truth.

Bear, who'd been sleeping nearby, hobbled to his feet.

Then Jack would find Bear and they'd leave together. They'd have to go slow, the two of them. It would be a long walk to Covington. The river would be their guide.

IN THE GROVE

CORA LEANED AGAINST the windowsill. Outside, the wind rustled the trees in the dark. She'd tried to sleep, but had gotten up sometime after two o'clock. She couldn't stop thinking of Jack and Nettie—of everything.

Nettie had given her back the journal and had asked her to stay after school. They'd sat in the yard in the shade of the trees. "I'm sorry I told on you," Nettie said, "but I got jealous when you made friends with that boy."

As confused as she'd been about Nettie's betrayal, Cora had realized in the last two weeks there were things about Nettie she hadn't missed. How Nettie had to be in charge. How her ideas were always the best. Jack was the one who had shown Cora this. He listened to her. He made no demands. "I don't want to fight, either," Cora said, "but if you want to be friends, you don't get to tell me how to behave. You don't get to decide who my friends are. Those are things I can choose for myself."

Nettie hadn't known what to say. Things between them weren't entirely better, but maybe, with time, they could be.

In the last days, so much had changed. Mr. Ogden was sick; the school board hadn't decided his future. Silas, Nana's oldest friend, was the long-ago boy who'd been blamed for the fire. And what a surprise that story about Mr. Graham had been!

Cora breathed in the sweet promise of rain. Would the clouds ever open? When?

Mostly, though, she thought of Jack. It had been three days since they'd found that story. Had Dr. Kingsbury discovered it missing? She'd wanted to check if Jack was all right, but she'd had to prepare for the Auxiliary Tea.

The shimmering world beckoned from outside. Wind swirled the curtains like an invitation. What if she went to Jack now? She could go to the grove to check on him. Cora took off her nightgown and pulled on her dress as the clock struck the half hour. She clung to the banister and crept down the stairs. As soon as she shut the door, she ran.

Her feet found their stride on the hard-packed earth. Cora raced through the alley and past Founder's Square, following the road out of town. Once she left the road, she pushed through the willows. It was dark and difficult to see, but the roar of the river led her to the grove. Ahead, a dark shape loomed nearby. Lightning flashed, exposing the wagon. Two blankets lay on the ground; one of them was empty.

The wind chilled Cora's skin.

She crept past the wagon. The sky blazed again. She saw someone walking the path to the river. Behind him was the old stray dog.

"Jack?" Cora ran to his side.

"What are you doing here?"

Bear barked and wagged his tail.

"Shhh." Jack stroked the dog's head. "We can't wake up Dr. Kingsbury."

"I had to be certain you were all right." Bear leaned against Cora's leg, his weight welcome and comforting. She ran her fingers over his snout. He lifted his head for more.

"Won't you get in trouble?" Jack said.

If she were found out, Cora couldn't imagine the trouble she'd be in. "No one will even notice I'm gone."

"Let's go where the doctor can't hear us, then." Jack took her to the rock where they'd hidden together after finding the story about Dr. Kingsbury. They climbed to the top. It was big enough for the two of them.

Though the thunder had weakened, the sky glimmered with pulses of light. There still was no sign of rain. Once it started, how long would it take to turn back the drought?

One storm wouldn't be enough. It could pour for weeks with little change.

Jack pulled his knees under his chin. "Cora," he said. "I'm not safe with the doctor. I'm going to run away."

An uncomfortable feeling twinged in her chest. She didn't know what to say, so Cora didn't bother with words. Instead she reached for Jack's hand. His fingers were cold, his palm rough with calluses.

"But I'm not going to go until after tomorrow. That wouldn't be right. First, I'm telling the truth at Founder's Day."

A flash of light cut the sky, revealing a man on the path. Cora slipped from the rock and crouched near the river.

"Jack?" Dr. Kingsbury called. "Jack!"

"I'm sorry," Jack whispered. "I have to go."

"If that boy thinks for a minute he—"

"Dr. Kingsbury, I'm here." Jack's feet hit the ground. "I couldn't sleep with the storm coming on."

"You stay near me, do you understand?"

Bear whined. There was a tussle and an intake of breath.

"I won't do it again," Jack said. "I promise."

Fear sliced through Cora with a sharp, swift edge, but this time she wouldn't stay hidden. She left the stone's shelter and followed the three of them at a distance. The doctor pulled Jack by his arm. Bear growled. Jack stumbled, trying to keep up.

"Call that dog off!" the doctor said.

Jack spoke to Bear with gentle words as the three of them neared the wagon.

"Now get some rest. I'll need you to sell the last of the tonic before we get out of town."

Jack pulled the blanket over his shoulders. Bear nestled at his back.

As soon as the doctor had settled, Cora left for the path to the road and raced through the outskirts of town. Branches scratched her skin. Brambles grabbed at her dress. She slowed as she neared McCalls' farm. A single light brightened the dark, a candle in a windowpane.

Cora knocked at the old farmhouse door. "Silas! Open up, please!" She knocked again, harder this time.

There was a shuffle of footsteps inside. The door opened a crack. "Who is it?"

"It's Cora. Please. I need your help." She told Silas everything that had happened, how worried she was about Jack. "Could you go? Could you watch him? Make sure he's safe?"

He touched her head tenderly. "Yes, child. Now go on home and get some sleep. I'll watch over Jack until the sun rises. I'll make sure he comes to no harm."

FOUNDER'S DAY

MISS MOORE WATCHED the children who led the parade, boys and girls dressed in blue waving colorful ribbons. Behind them were drums, marking time for the trumpets, the brass horns alight with the sun. Horses came next, their heads bobbing together, with silk flowers entwined in their bridles. Last of all was a wagon draped in bunting that carried Nathanael James.

There he was. The mayor, but she couldn't go to him. Miss Moore would have to wait.

She knew Founder's Day always started like this, with its crowds and its stalls of sweet-smelling cakes. The clouds hadn't kept people away. It wasn't yet raining, but it had to storm soon. It was only a matter of time.

She'd never come to the parade before. Every year before this one, Miss Moore drew her curtains and had tried to settle her mind with a book. Though she always looked forward to a day lost to reading, she never got very far. The commotion outside pulled her back to the window, where she'd end up watching the parade below.

Two days ago, the Auxiliary Tea had ended not long after she'd arrived. She'd thought of it often—not its strange talk of a fire—but how good it had felt being with others, if only for a little time. Miss Moore had forgotten how nice it was to have a bit of company. Afterward, she'd gone in search of Mayor James to tell him what she'd learned of the doctor. He wasn't at City Hall, she was told, but in the grove with Dr. Kingsbury. She hardly could go to him then. Yesterday, she'd stayed in bed, too dizzy to stand on her feet.

Today she'd decided she'd watch the parade. Maybe she'd catch the mayor afterward. Miss Moore had left home early enough that she'd found a choice spot to see the procession—the corner where Main Street ended and Founder's Square began.

Children darted and ran as they snacked on cookies. She nudged a bottle out of the way. It rolled from the sidewalk onto the street. Nearby, a redheaded man nodded in greeting. Beside him a woman cradled a baby. The Muellers, that's who they were, the ones who sold furniture not far from the millinery. Last spring, a young Mueller had pressed his face against her shop window. His father had insisted he clean every pane once he learned of the mess the boy made.

Mayor James waved to the crowd as his wagon rolled by. He looked sturdy and strong in his brown linen suit, his mustache neatly trimmed. He held a piece of polished wood, long as a ruler, thick as a wrist. The wood was from the tree, no doubt, though she didn't know its history.

As the last of the parade entered the square, the children with ribbons surrounded the stage under the Great Oak Tree. Rows of bottles rimmed its sides, even more than the dozens scattered on Main Street. Nearby was Kingsbury's wagon and Jack, the boy who knew the man's secrets. She thought of Ernest and the other boy, Isaac. As soon as she could, she'd find Mayor James.

Where was that man who called himself a doctor? Miss Moore had heard it said in her shop that he'd play a part in today's celebration.

She followed as the crowd pressed closer, stopping not very far from the stage. Near the front was a group carrying burning lanterns, as though it were the dead of night. Behind them, others held up signs: *Alcohol the Destroyer. Wine Is a Mocker. Lips That Touch Liquor Shall Never Touch*

Mine! Around her, some clutched bottles of tonic with even more sticking out of their pockets. It took all sorts of people to make a world, Mother once had said. Miss Moore sighed. All sorts indeed.

She lifted her eyes to the oak tree. Her bonnet still dangled from a branch high above, though now it was missing its feather. The plume must have gotten caught up in the wind. She pictured it stuck to the slats of a fence, the tip of the feather dirtied and bent. Miss Moore rubbed her temples, not because of any pain, but because she'd been feeling so dizzy.

Mayor James's wagon pulled to a stop. He climbed to the stage and turned to the crowd. The children with ribbons sat in the grass. A silence fell over the gathering.

Miss Moore kept her gaze on her hat in the oak, hoping no one would notice how stupid she felt, how ridiculously out of place. Moments like this were what she expected from a town so bent on tradition. What she hadn't predicted was the quiver rising in her chest. A stirring sensation, like an awakening seed, the same feeling she'd had at the Auxiliary Tea.

The mayor began. "Father of Oakdale. Faithful founder. There's no better way to describe Robert Frasier. He gave us the oak that gives us our name. His early devotion grew our town into what it's become today. As we start our Founder's Day celebrations, may we never forget Oakdale's first friend."

Mayor James folded his hands. "Elijah Kingsbury, please join me onstage."

The man who was wanted by the Wabash police climbed the stage in his coat of impeccable black. He carried himself like he'd always been a part of the day's festivities.

"I have to believe," Mayor James said, "if Robert Frasier were with us today, he'd call Dr. Kingsbury our town's newest friend."

Mr. Mueller sneered. "He's no friend of mine."

A few people looked at him curiously.

His wife shifted the child she held. "Tobias, hold your tongue. You know the tonic helped the baby."

"In the two weeks he's been here," the mayor went on, "Dr. Kingsbury has taken great care with our town."

A roll of thunder rumbled and cracked. Miss Moore tugged the strings of her bonnet, making sure they were firm beneath her chin. Everyone looked to the darkening clouds. Within minutes, they'd turned bold and angry. She swayed a little on her feet. If only there were a place she could sit. Perhaps that would help her feel better.

The mayor held up the stick of wood. "This came from a branch of the Great Oak Tree that fell during the storm of 1804. Like the tree, Oakdale's been battered again. Not from wind this time, but from drought."

A drop of rain splashed Miss Moore's cheek. Another fell in her palm.

Kingsbury's hair swept over his brow. He raised his arms like a conductor, the people of Oakdale his symphony. "It's time," he cried out. "Time to call down the rain!"

Did anyone notice the look of him, like a snake ready to strike?

"All of you who've bought bottles to hasten the storm, open them. Hold them up!"

Hands lifted throughout the crowd in a cresting wave of glass.

"Call the rains down with the tonic!"

Cheers rose up, hearty and loud.

A clap of thunder shook the skies. A spatter of rain drifted down. Miss Moore turned her face to the mist softly brushing her cheeks. Shouts of joy tore through the square and traveled the edges of Main Street. A drop of rain slipped from her chin and puddled in the dip of her neck.

The stirring fluttered inside her again, like a sprout in search of the sun. Next to her, the Muellers embraced. The baby beamed with a gummy grin. Miss Moore couldn't help but smile back.

For three Founder's Days she'd kept to herself. Perhaps that had been a mistake.

"Praise the heavens!" the mayor said. "It's the miracle we've all waited for."

Kingsbury walked the length of the stage. "We must

nurture this rain," he shouted, "as a gardener tends a vine. We must encourage it to grow in power!"

Mr. Mueller scowled. "He means we should buy more tonic."

The doctor raised his bottle high. "A vigorous storm is what this town needs."

Miss Moore's head spun; she fought not to stumble. Black spots clouded her vision. What was happening? She reached for Mr. Mueller's arm.

He stared at her in confusion. "Are you quite all right, Miss Moore?"

Her knees buckled. He lowered her down. "Help!" he shouted. "I need assistance!"

Miss Moore felt herself being lifted. It seemed as though she sailed through the crowd. Carefully, she was set on the stage. Before the darkness overtook her, she heard the kind voice of Alma James. "It will be all right, Miss Moore. Dr. Kingsbury's here."

THE BOY HE'D ONCE BEEN

THE MOON BATHED the field in luminance, a beauty like Silas had never seen. The barn cast a shadow over the grass, the only true darkness that night. He wished he'd realized it would be his last with his friend Evangeline.

They'd talked of the weeks they'd spent as friends and how long he might stay in town. "What I like about you," Evangeline said, "is that you're loyal and kind." She leaned her head on Silas's shoulder and watched the moon as it rose ever higher. "Promise me someday you'll come back, and when you do, you'll look for me."

Then the fire had raged. Silas had stayed away, unsure what Evangeline thought of the rumors.

Even so, Silas had kept his word. Every time he'd come

back to Oakdale, he'd walked near McCalls', hoping to catch sight of her. But in all those years, he'd never seen her again.

— ◇ —

SILAS SET DOWN the board he carried as the rain began to fall. The rain dripped from his hair and wetted his skin, a glorious reprieve from the heat.

Last night, he'd been unable to sleep, so he'd sat with his memories. He'd thought of Evangeline and his shame because of the barn and its burning. He'd believed coming back and rebuilding the barn would heal him of that burden. The barn was well underway, but so far nothing inside him had changed.

Then Cora had come in the dark of the night. She'd told him the doctor's boy was in danger. He'd gone to the grove to keep watch over him. A boy like Silas had been once. A child with no support in this town except for Cora, his friend.

Silas had watched from his hiding place beneath a willow tree. Sometimes the boy stirred under his blanket or the old dog shifted in his sleep. For a time, the boy sat up, unmoving. It seemed he was staring straight into the willow where Silas had hidden himself. Of course the boy couldn't see him, but as Jack sat, stroking the dog, Silas felt a connection to the child, as though he were watching his younger self. As if he and Jack had made an agreement.

As the boy settled to sleep again, Silas had whispered, "Don't you worry." He'd stayed until daybreak, when the boy and the doctor had left for Founder's Day. In the crowd, the boy would be fine, Silas reasoned. The doctor wouldn't dare harm him then. After the show, he'd find the boy. He'd offer him work and a safe place to stay.

The pile of boards glistened with rain. How strange that, after a night of no sleep, Silas could feel as refreshed as he did. The rain was a part of it, of course, and the memories of Evangeline. She'd believed in him when no one else had. It was enough to keep him going. Silas figured if he kept at his work, the barn would be finished a few months from now.

Thunder rolled, deep and distant. He heard the faint sound of voices raised. The rain must have reached Founder's Square, where they were holding the day's festivities.

Silas set his last board aside. *"What I like about you,"* Evangeline had said, *"is that you're loyal and kind."* He thought of the boy with no one to help and his peace which had been forestalled.

His returning to Oakdale wasn't what he'd first thought. He'd come for another reason.

The show would end soon. He'd better get going. Silas crossed the field and climbed into his wagon. "Don't you worry, Jack," he said aloud.

He'd returned not for his own young self but for this other child.

A WORTHLESS CURE

HAD MISS MOORE fainted or had something worse happened? From the wagon, Jack strained to see her chest rise, but it was impossible to tell. Mrs. James sat beside Miss Moore, her skirt fanned over the stage.

The crowd was a sea of sound. Dr. Kingsbury hurried to the woman's side. He pressed a bottle to her lips. The tonic spilled, covering the stage and forming a puddle that shimmered with rain. The doctor lifted Miss Moore's head and offered it again.

"He's not a doctor," Jack said. Some nearby turned to see who was speaking. Jack ran from the wagon and pushed through the crowd. "Stop!" he shouted, but his voice disappeared in the noise around him. His legs wavered as he climbed to the stage.

"Do something!" Mrs. James said to the doctor.

Dr. Kingsbury bent over Miss Moore, his dark hair hiding his face.

"Mrs. James?" Jack called. "Dr. Kingsbury can't help. He isn't a doctor like he says."

But she hadn't heard over the clamoring crowd and the steady beat of the rain.

Jack took a deep breath, as the doctor had taught him. For two weeks he'd told the people of Oakdale the doctor was a man to be trusted. Who would listen now? "Someone else needs to help Miss Moore. Dr. Kingsbury is a fraud."

This time his voice carried. Slowly, the crowd made sense of the words. Some nodded their heads, but most were shocked, staring in disbelief. Jack found Cora, off to one side. She wove through the crowd and pushed to the front, until she was close to the stage.

The doctor's eyes settled on him, cold and piercing.

Jack swallowed. He wouldn't let fear overtake him.

"The boy speaks nonsense," the doctor said. He held his hand to Mrs. James. "Come now, help me lift Miss Moore's shoulders. Then I'll try again with the tonic."

Jack stepped over the puddle of medicine, blocking the doctor's way.

Miss Moore's head lolled to one side, her face drained of all color.

"Bring some water," Jack said. "That's what she needs." He remembered Miss Moore buying tonic. Had the medicine not agreed with her? Once, in southern Ohio, a man had been ill after trying some. It was after he'd drunk a cupful of water that he'd started to feel like himself again.

"Here! I've got it." The mayor brought a bucket from the back of the stage. Jack filled the dipper and held it out to Miss Moore. "Please, you need to drink."

The woman's eyes fluttered, but she didn't respond. Mrs. James plunged her hand into the bucket and washed it over Miss Moore's face.

"The tonic will help," the doctor said. "The tonic will awaken her." He shoved the bucket aside and pushed the bottle to her mouth.

"No," Jack said. "Leave her alone."

Dr. Kingsbury's eyes narrowed, but Jack refused to look away.

"Alma," Mayor James said, "if I call for a wagon, would you go with Miss Moore? Set her up in Nettie's room. She can stay as long as she needs."

"Yes," Mrs. James said. "Absolutely."

The men who'd lifted Miss Moore onstage carried her

to the bunting-draped wagon. Mrs. James climbed in. The crowd moved aside as the wagon rolled past.

"What happened, Dr. Kingsbury?" The tips of the mayor's ears had gone a deep red. "Why didn't your tonic help Miss Moore?"

The doctor's wet hair stuck to his face. He tried to brush it away. "Because her faith wasn't strong enough. She must not have trusted the tonic would help."

"No," Jack said for a second time. "Dr. Kingsbury's not telling the truth. Mayor James, you have to believe me."

"Then what's the truth, Jack, if you're so certain?" The doctor's dark eyes filled with warning.

Watch yourself. I mean it. Jack remembered the pain that had seared his arm as the doctor threatened his life. But he owed the people of Oakdale the truth. "I know your real name is Elijah Barry. That you performed with Dun's Theatrical Troupe when you claimed you were selling your medicine."

"It's true, Uncle Nathanael," Cora called out from the front of the stage. "You can believe what he says. Jack and I found an article the doctor keeps hidden."

Rain drenched Jack's shirt and dripped from his sleeves. He looked at Cora gratefully. Then he raised his voice, loud enough to ensure everyone in the crowd could hear over the storm. "I know two boys have gone missing, and Dr. Kingsbury had something to do with it."

A strange hush fell over the square.

In an instant, the doctor leaped from the stage.

"Catch him!" Mayor James said. "Don't let him get away!"

LET THE BOY SPEAK

THE DOCTOR DISAPPEARED in the crowd, Mr. Mueller racing after him. Through the rain, Jack spied the doctor's coat, a shadow pushing against the throng. He ran down the steps to follow.

"Grab him!" Mr. Mueller shouted.

There was a thump and a splash.

Dr. Kingsbury lay sprawled in the mud. Mr. Mueller grabbed the doctor's shoulders and yanked him to his feet.

"It's over," Mr. Mueller said, tightening his grip on the doctor. "You're not going anywhere now."

Jack stared at the man he'd trusted completely. Dr. Kingsbury's suit was splattered with muck. A scrape reddened his chin.

A white-bearded man in a checkered shirt grasped the doctor's arm. "Let's take him back to the mayor," he said.

Before Lu had gotten sick, Jack had caught an enormous trout. He'd fought to pull it to the bank, but the fish had thrashed, and in the last moment, jerked itself free from the hook. It had slipped through the water, a splash of pink marking its speckled sides.

"How'd you do it?" someone shouted, as the men dragged the doctor back to the stage. "How'd you make Henry walk again?"

"I spent two dollars on tonic," another yelled. "I want back every penny!"

"We'll get to that," Mr. Mueller said, "but first we let the boy speak."

Like the fish, Jack was free. He owed Dr. Kingsbury nothing.

Jack followed the men up the stage steps. Dr. Kingsbury hung his head, wet hair covering his face. His skin was ashen, as though he were ailing, his body so slender it seemed fragile and weak. He'd once held such power over Jack, but not anymore. Jack wasn't afraid. Turning his back to the doctor, he spoke to the restless crowd. "Another boy used to work for the doctor. His name was Isaac Blum."

"Shut your mouth!" Dr. Kingsbury said. He fought against the men, who held him fast.

But Jack wasn't bound to the doctor now. "The day we arrived in Oakdale, Isaac disappeared. You can ask Mr. Ogden about it."

"I told you," the doctor said, "Isaac left on his own."

Jack remembered the salute, the signal Isaac gave him in every new town. It had meant it was time to get to work, a promise they'd meet again soon.

"No," Jack said, "he didn't. I found his pack hidden not far from the grove. I looked for him. A couple of times. I went to Greenville to check with his cousin, but she hadn't seen Isaac, either." Rain ran down Jack's face. "He's not the only missing boy. There's another, named Ernest McPherson."

Dr. Kingsbury whipped his head around. "Where did you learn that name?"

Jack ignored him, continuing on. "Dr. Kingsbury's wanted in Wabash, Indiana, the town where Miss Moore is from. Six years ago, Ernest went missing. He'd worked as a stagehand the summer the theater troupe came to town. When the police located the troupe, they discovered the doctor had already run."

"What would you know about any of that?" Dr. Kingsbury said.

"I heard it from Miss Moore. Ask her, Mayor James, when she's feeling better." If she got better. Jack hoped she would soon. "The newspaper editor in Greenville probably knows something, too." Jack's fingers fumbled as he tried to unroll the scrap of paper he'd found. "But Isaac was the first to tell me. Here." He held up the strip. *Ernest McPherson*, it said. The name had been written in faded blue ink. Two lines underscored the letter *c*. Isaac hadn't told him directly, but Jack had to believe, if given the chance, Isaac would have confided in him.

Isaac. A twist of pain cut through Jack's chest.

Dr. Kingsbury strained against those who held him.

Jack hardly noticed the rain streaming down. "I know Isaac didn't run away. I know it because you killed him. Isaac. You took his life. How could you do it?"

The doctor sneered. "I didn't do anything the boy didn't deserve."

"I've heard enough from you, Kingsbury!" Mayor James said. "Take him to the jail in Greenville. Tell the sheriff everything."

Mr. Mueller took off his belt and used it to bind the doctor's wrists. A group of men led the doctor away. Some in the crowd jeered as he passed. A bottle of tonic flew through the air, striking the doctor's back.

Cora rushed onto the stage and ran to Jack's side. "I'm so sorry about Isaac." She brushed her fingers over his wrist where the bruises once had been. "Oh, Jack. I'm so glad you're all right."

Apart from the time she'd reached for his hand, the

only kind touch he'd had since home had come from the old stray dog. A memory washed over him: His parents holding him close. Lucy's arms wrapped around his knees. It was right before he'd said goodbye and gone with Dr. Kingsbury.

All at once, he realized he wanted to leave. "Is there anyone who can take me home?"

"I will," the man with the beard and the checkered shirt said. He'd stayed behind as the others had left with the doctor.

"Jack," Cora said, "this is Silas."

"I'd be happy to help. Where are you from?"

"Not far from here. A little town called Covington."

Silas stared. "Now, isn't that interesting. I lived in Covington when I was a boy. I'll take you home in the morning," he said, "once this storm has passed."

Jack inhaled the clean scent of rain. Shop windows winked as water slid over them. The oak's leaves had deepened and started to fade. So much had changed in the last two weeks. "Cora," he said, "could you come in the morning?" He wouldn't leave town without saying goodbye.

BENT AND BROKEN

THE STORM RAGED into the night. Waves of rain pelted the shops. Water poured from overfilled gutters, tumbling bottles of tonic. It coursed over the rooftops in cascading torrents, turning the street to a river of mud.

No one was out but the old black dog, who hid in the back of the alley. It had taken hours for him to reach town, long enough that once he'd arrived, the streets were deserted. His boy was gone.

A flash of lightning pierced the gloom. A rumble rattled the windowpanes.

If the dog hadn't cowered in the narrow alley, he would have witnessed the Great Oak sway. The dog would have seen its branches quake as the tree crashed to the ground.

Only a portion of the oak's trunk remained, split open and charred in its middle.

The storm lashed and raged for hours. Later, when the rains diminished, the dog crept from his hiding place. He lifted his snout to the nighttime air. He smelled the drenched earth and the blackened wood and the sharp scent of the tonic.

The oak lay broken with branches bent. Its sodden red leaves littered the ground. Skirting the tree, the dog kept his distance. It was time for him to return to the river, though each step jarred his aching hip. He needed to find his boy again.

A SIMPLE REQUEST

LIGHTNING FLICKERED AT the window. Miss Moore sat up in a dimly lit room in a bed she'd never seen. She wore a fresh linen dressing gown. A candle burned on the nightstand beside her.

"Where am I?"

"At my house," Alma James said. She sat nearby in a rocking chair. Her dress, usually perfect, was rumpled and torn. Dirt smudged her cheeks. "You fainted at Founder's Day."

Rain pounded the windows in the dark night. The sound was welcome after months of drought. It reminded Miss Moore of her childhood days. When storms would come, she and her mother would sit together in front of a fire. They would sew in the firelight, listening as rain pattered on the roof.

Miss Moore rubbed her temples, the dizziness gone. "I've been taking the tonic. It helped with my headaches. But I wonder if something in the medicine left me feeling unwell."

Alma James scooted the rocker closer, into the ring of candlelight. "I'm so glad you're feeling better, Miss Moore. You've given us quite a scare. It wouldn't surprise me if it was the tonic. The doctor's been named a fraud."

"What?"

Alma rested her hand on Miss Moore's. "The doctor's boy told the crowd everything. He said there were two missing boys, one of them from your hometown."

"Ernest," she whispered. "I tried to find the mayor and tell him, but—"

Alma squeezed her hand gently. "Don't you worry yourself, Miss Moore. The man's been arrested and taken to Greenville."

Miss Moore settled herself on the pillows. This town had been cold to her from the beginning. She'd been snubbed and ignored. But in the last years, something had changed. Slowly, a kindness had grown, much of it from Alma James.

Why had she taken so long to acknowledge it?

"Alma." A whisper of embarrassment overtook Miss Moore in saying the woman's name. It was so personal. Intimate. What one would call a friend. She sat up higher and straightened her back. Eloise Moore tried again. "Alma," she said. "I wish you'd use my given name. Please. Call me Eloise."

STILL THE SAME

WALTER OGDEN STARED at the emptiness left in the rain-washed sky. How was it possible the Great Oak was gone?

As a boy, he'd wanted to reach through the fence, not to climb the oak, but simply to touch it. He'd thought running his fingers over the bark would somehow fill him with courage. His whole life the oak had been a constant in the stark months of winter and the lushness of spring. A familiar presence. A symbol of community.

Others who'd heard the crash in the night had come to the square, too. Together, they spoke in hushed tones. Some wiped away tears as they embraced.

"Excuse me, Mr. Ogden. May I have a word?" Mr.

Brindley peered through his spectacles. "I know it's a strange time to talk about this, but I wanted to tell you as soon as I could. The school board would like to keep you on. While the palsy might present some challenges, we're firm in believing you can still teach."

Last night, Mr. Ogden hadn't slept as the rain pounded against the roof. He'd lit the lamp and sat on his bed. As he'd done many times since he'd first seen the tremor, Walter Ogden studied his hands. While the right one stayed calm, his left hand quaked.

Mr. Brindley lowered his head. "I admit this wasn't our first inclination. Your students. They changed our minds."

The children had helped Walter, too, had shown him he wasn't damaged or broken. Palsy or not, he was still the same man. An illness wouldn't define him. Last night, as rain slicked the windowpanes, he'd thought of the lessons he still wanted to teach. Why should he stop if he wasn't yet ready? "Thank you, Mr. Brindley. Give my thanks to the board. I'd be honored to continue at Oakdale School."

Many who'd gathered in the square lingered near the fallen oak, close enough to touch the tree if they wanted, though no one dared to reach out a hand. Mr. Ogden watched the mayor examine the tree, surveying the damage the storm had caused. "How much can you salvage?" the man asked Mr. Mueller.

"Enough to make a bench or a door."

"A door," Mayor James said. "For City Hall."

The oak's destruction didn't feel real, no more believable than what had happened yesterday. Mr. Ogden had seen it unfold on the stage: Dr. Kingsbury's downfall, the boy's bravery. The doctor had been called a charlatan, a revelation that had cut neat and quick, like a paper's edge slicing the skin. Then more had been revealed: The man was a murderer, a vile creature who'd taken two innocent lives. Mr. Ogden hadn't imagined the second boy; there had been another assistant.

Mayor James lifted the piece of wood, a signal he wanted to speak. "My neighbors and friends, the last day has been difficult. I'm sorry for all that has happened. I hope you can learn to trust me again. Dr. Kingsbury has been taken to Greenville. I've sent word to the authorities in Wabash, Indiana, on the direction of our own Miss Moore."

The mayor tapped the oak's trunk with the piece of wood. "The Great Oak's gone but it won't be forgotten. I've asked Mr. Mueller to fashion a door to display in City Hall. The tree will live on in our memories, in the stories we tell our children. Come, everyone, take a piece of the tree—a twig, a leaf, a strip of bark. May it be your reminder of how deep our roots grow."

Mr. Ogden pressed his palm to the oak. Even now there was power running through it. What he hadn't known when he was a child was what the fence was really for. It wasn't to shore up Oakdale's strength but to hold back the threat of harm. From fire, from outsiders—anything that might damage or cause injury. But the fence hadn't stopped the lightning bolt. In wanting protection, Oakdale had closed itself off, as he had done by retreating from everyone these last weeks.

As much as he loved the old oak, perhaps it was good, its coming down, for the sake of his community. Maybe, somehow, the tree's destruction offered Oakdale a chance at a new beginning.

Nearby, Cora snapped a twig from a branch. When she spied Mr. Ogden, she shyly waved as if she hadn't seen him in weeks.

His foot made it difficult to walk, but he was in no hurry to reach her. "Thank you, Cora, for believing in me."

"I was only telling the truth," she said.

"I've been thinking about some lessons we might try in the spring."

"In the spring?" Cora's eyes brightened. "Does that mean you're not leaving?"

"I'm not going anywhere." It felt good to say it aloud.

Cora threw her arms around him. Mr. Ogden hugged her back.

A SECOND CHANCE

"NOT MUCH FARTHER now, Nana." Cora held her grandmother's hand as they walked through the fields on the outskirts of town. Father had brought them to the end of the road before leaving for work that morning.

"I'm fine, my dear. Don't you worry about me."

Though Nana moved slowly, her steps were sure. Cora hoped they'd reach McCalls' on time. An hour ago, when she'd awakened, the skies had been clear, but now clouds hung at the edges. In no time it would rain again.

"Where are we going?" Nana asked. Cora had told her last night, after the talk with Mother and Father. She'd reminded Nana before they'd left home. "There's a friend of mine I want you to meet."

At first, Mother had been hesitant—Cora and Nana going alone to meet an old friend and the doctor's boy—but Father had insisted on it. "Think about what our girl has done. She helped the boy bring down that doctor. Now your mother can see her oldest friend. Lauren, you can't keep them from this."

In the end, Mother had given her blessing. This morning, she'd sent them all off with a kiss.

McCalls' fence came into view, then the fields with their asters and goldenrod and the farmhouse with the porch caved in. Just beyond was the beginnings of the new barn. But where was the wagon? Had they already left?

"Nana, could you wait for a moment? I need to be certain my friend is still here." She left Nana near the fence, under the shade of a tree. Cora slipped through the rails and started to run. Hopefully, the wagon was parked around back. She rounded the side of the old farmhouse and saw Silas and Jack in the wagon seat. Silas gripped the reins, as though ready to go. Bear stood in the wagon bed.

"Wait!"

Silas turned.

Cora stopped, catching her breath. "Please don't go yet."

"I told you," Jack said. "I told you she'd come." A dimple formed in his cheek as he smiled.

"I'm sorry, Cora. We waited a bit, but I didn't want to be caught in the rain."

She thought of Nana's words at the tea, that Silas was her oldest friend. "Before I tell Jack goodbye, there's someone I want you to meet. Could you bring the wagon around to the spot where the fence reaches the tree?"

Silas shaded his eyes and gazed near the fence. He didn't ask Cora who waited there. A strange look came over him—a pinch of caution mixed up with hope. "All right," Silas said. "How about you climb in the back."

The wagon rolled through the sweet-smelling grass. At the fence, Cora and Jack jumped down. "Who is it?" Jack asked.

"You'll have to wait and see."

Nana rested against the tree's slender trunk, her white tasseled shawl over her shoulders.

"Nana," Cora said. "This is my friend Jack, the boy Nettie mentioned at the tea." There was no need to say more. What Nettie had done didn't matter now.

"Oh, Jack," Nana said. "It's lovely to meet you."

Cora watched Silas ease himself from the wagon. "But Jack's not the reason I brought you here."

Nana lifted her eyes to the man coming toward them. Would Nana recognize him, with his silvery beard, as the boy he used to be?

"I want you to meet someone. My nana. Her name is Evangeline."

"Evangeline," he repeated, as if the name meant everything. "I hoped it was you." His voice was gruff, like it stuck in his throat. "I've come back, just like I promised. I came a whole lot of times, but I never was able to find you."

Nana's brows pinched together. "Have we met before?"

"Yes," Cora said. "When you were a girl. This is Silas, your oldest friend."

Nana's eyes warmed. Tears formed in their corners. "You're the boy from McCalls'. I told everyone you didn't set the fire, but no one would believe me."

"You did that? For me?" Silas wrapped his hands around hers. "Thank you, Evangeline."

Nana smiled. How much she understood, Cora couldn't tell, but there was no denying her happiness.

Silas looked overhead. "The rain's coming soon. We'd better get going."

"Cora." Jack held out his hand. "This is for you. To remember me by." He gave her the wooden carving of Bear, one ear longer than the other, its tail jagged and nicked.

She cradled the carving in her palm. "But you made this for Lucy."

"I'm bringing Bear home. He'll be more than enough for the two of us."

"Write me a letter," Cora said as Jack climbed to the wagon seat.

"I will, as soon as I'm home."

"I'll send you one every week!"

Silas got in the seat beside him. "I'll bring Jack around every now and then, if his parents think it's all right."

"Maybe," Cora asked, "maybe sometime you could take me there?" There was so much of the world she wanted to see. What better way than to see it with Jack? "And of course, I'll bring Nana by, too, if that's all right with you, Silas."

"Can't think of anything better," he said.

Cora climbed to the top of the fence and sat on the highest beam.

Jack waved as Silas flicked the reins. Nana slipped her arm around Cora's waist. The wagon jerked forward, and Cora felt her eyes fill, from sadness but also from gratitude. How could she have known, when the doctor arrived, she'd meet such a boy? A boy who'd become her friend.

BETTER DAYS

IN THE LATE afternoon, they came to a barn, a timeworn building that had faded to brown. Its weathered walls leaned to one side. Jack had seen it hundreds of times. "Here's where you turn," he told Silas.

"Is it?" Silas shook his head. "That's the same turn to my old place."

More than a year had passed since Jack left, but little in the land had changed. He knew every tree by the sweep of its branches, remembered each bump in the road. The sun, low in the sky, washed the fields with rosy light.

They'd traveled most of the day in silence. Quiet could be uncomfortable, and sometimes Jack worried when he couldn't fill it. This silence, though, was easy and warm, welcome as a quilt on a winter night. Only once had Silas chosen to talk, sometime after they'd stopped to eat.

"Friday night, Cora came to my door. She said you'd had trouble with Dr. Kingsbury and worried you might come to some harm. I went to the grove to check on you."

A tingling sensation washed over Jack's skin. "Were you in the willows?" he asked. He'd felt a presence that night. Jack had sat up when he couldn't sleep, so nervous about what the doctor might do, he'd pretended someone was watching nearby, looking out for him.

"I was. Stayed on until you left for the square."

Someone had watched him. Someone had cared. Two someones—Cora and Silas.

The road twisted and curved and straightened again. Jack's heart quickened as they neared the front yard.

Silas stared. "I know this place. It's the farm where I lived when I was a boy."

"You did?" Jack said. "When was that?"

Silas held the reins loose in his hands. "We'd had a terrible summer. There'd been no rain for weeks. I went to Oakdale to take on some work, a boy not much older than you."

Again a prickling crept up Jack's arms. Silas had worked in Oakdale, too. Cora's nana had befriended him. How similar their two lives had been.

He could see Ma near the laundry basket pinning

a sheet on the line. Behind her, Lucy skipped through the grass.

Ma looked up as the wagon slowed. She had sunburned cheeks and sand-colored lashes—same as she'd always had. "Jack?" The sheet she held fell to the ground. Bear barked as she crushed Jack in a hug. "You're home. It's so good to see you!"

"Jack! My Jack!" Lucy yelled as she ran. Jack scooped her up in his arms. Lu reached for Bear in the wagon bed; the dog covered her face with kisses.

Papa came from the barn, hat low on his brow, a blue bandanna tied at his neck. "Where's Dr. Kingsbury?" he asked.

"He's been taken to jail in Greenville," Jack said. He told his parents everything. How the doctor wasn't who he'd claimed, how he'd lied about his tonic. How Isaac had gone missing two weeks ago and the doctor had taken his life.

Ma held Jack close and wouldn't let go as Lucy chased Bear in the yard. "We trusted that man. I'm so glad you're all right. What would we have done if you had been harmed?"

"Your boy was brave," Silas said. "He stood up to Kingsbury. I wish you could have seen it."

Papa shook Silas's hand. "Thank you for bringing him home."

Jack pulled away from his mother. "Silas says he lived on this farm, back when he was a boy."

"Did you now?" Papa said. "My grandfather bought this place years ago, not long after that terrible drought."

"It's that drought that took our family away."

"Silas," Jack said. "You need to come back."

"Yes." Papa nodded. "Anytime."

Lucy squeezed Jack's legs in a hug. He kissed the top of her curly head. It was good to be home, where he belonged.

There were things he wished he could change. How the doctor had deceived and used him. How he hadn't known of the danger Isaac had faced. But not everything could be doctored or fixed.

In time he'd write to Jennie Blum. He'd tell her how sorry he was and ask if he could come visit. He'd do his best to share his memories with someone who'd loved Isaac, too.

There was something Dr. Kingsbury had taught him that Jack knew was true. Hope was what bound people together. It kept a soul going, promising better days.

"Jack," Silas said, reaching down from the wagon. He grasped Jack's fingers in his rough hand. "I want to thank you for what you've done."

"Thank me? What for?" Jack looked into the man's weathered face with eyes a color he couldn't quite name.

"I carried a burden from my younger days. You've helped me to release it."

Jack didn't know what Silas meant, but he was starting to be all right with things he didn't understand: How the

Great Oak had grown in the span of a season. How Silas's boyhood mirrored his own. How a girl he hadn't known two weeks ago was now his friend.

Miracles, every one of them.

"Next time I see you, I'll have Cora with me," Silas said as he flicked the reins.

Lucy grabbed Jack's hand as the wagon left. "Come, Jack. Let's play."

He remembered the promise he'd made to himself, that he'd give Lu the time and attention she needed. She tugged him again, ready to go.

"Can we play for a bit?" he asked his parents.

Ma smiled. "Go on."

Jack and Lucy raced toward the hill where the river lay, the dog Bear trailing behind.

AUTHOR'S NOTE

Medical knowledge has come a long way since the 1800s. Back then, far less was understood about illness and the human body. Because medical training was limited, treatments varied widely. It was easy for anyone with a little experience to claim to be a doctor—and some did, for their own personal gain.

People who deceive others to benefit themselves are called charlatans, quacks, frauds, or con men. During the nineteenth century, charlatans found plenty of willing customers in the rural regions of the United States (90 percent of the country then) where doctors were scarce. Most families at that time relied on home remedies that helped ease the discomfort of minor illnesses but were no match for serious diseases or chronic conditions. Lack of medical knowledge, limited access to proper care, and ineffective home remedies were the perfect combination for the rise of patent medicines.

Patent medicines, sometimes called cure-alls, were unregulated medications with over-the-top claims that they could fix any ailment. Anyone with a bit of skill, a little medical insight, and a strong business sense could create and sell a cure-all. These "medicines" came in a variety of forms. Tonics and tinctures were meant to be swallowed. Liniments and salves were applied to the skin. Some self-described doctors moved from town to town to sell their products, a spectacle called the traveling medicine show. These shows were part entertainment, part lecture, and part doctor's visit.

Many people viewed the traveling doctor as an authority figure. They fell under the spell of hypnotic speeches and demonstrations that were meant to deceive. Like Dr. Kingsbury, a man named Lefty McClair claimed he could restore hearing. He added a few drops of his "medicine" to a person's ear and then rubbed it vigorously. Lefty McClair wasn't curing deafness. He was removing impacted earwax! But what mattered to Lefty—and what his audience saw—was the sudden change the medicine produced. This was "proof" of its power and demonstrated Lefty was a man to be trusted.

Did patent medicines really work? This is a tricky

question. Some patent medicines "may have had medical value, provided they were taken in the right doses for the appropriate ailment."[1] Some people improved because of the "placebo effect," a phenomenon where recovery comes from simply believing a medicine can heal.[2] Many patent medicines included addictive substances such as alcohol, opium, morphine, and even cocaine. These substances could mask an ailment, bringing temporary relief. And perhaps most important to remember, when given enough time, the human body often heals itself of minor illnesses.

Dr. Elijah Kingsbury was not a real man but is loosely based on John Austen Hamlin. Hamlin was a struggling magician who sold a liniment he claimed gave anyone the power to perform magic tricks. This promise left Hamlin with unhappy customers, but he found unexpected success when a man insisted Hamlin's Wizard Oil had healed his rheumatism. Hamlin saw the man's words as an opportunity. Soon he insisted his oil not only healed rheumatism, but pneumonia, hydrophobia, lame backs, asthma, sore throats, toothaches, headaches, stiff joints, and even cancer. Hamlin's Wizard Oil contained camphor, turpentine, ammonia, cloves, and alcohol—ingredients certain to make the skin tingle. That warm sensation when rubbed on the

1. Anderson, Anne. *Snake Oil, Hustlers, and Hambones: The American Medicine Show.* Jefferson, North Carolina: McFarland and Co. Inc., 2000.

2. Placebos, also called sugar pills, are still used today in medical testing.

skin could convince a person the oil was working. Imagine the burn Hamlin's Wizard Oil would have caused if swallowed![3] Hamlin sent troupes of performers dressed in long frock coats to towns where they entertained audiences for weeks and sold Wizard Oil from a wagon.

The underlined sections Jack finds in Dr. Kilmer's book are actual claims from various patent medicines:

- Burdock Blood Bitters claimed to cure "all disorders arising from impure blood or a deranged liver."
- Dr. Kilmer's Swamp Root Kidney, Liver, and Bladder Cure worked on "pimples, diabetes," or "internal slime fever."
- Kilmer's Ocean Weed Remedy could be used to cure "sudden death."
- Hamlin's Wizard Oil stated, "There's no sore it will not heal, no pain it will not subdue."
- Kickapoo Indian Sagwa claimed, "If you are not feeling just right and cannot locate the trouble, take this wonderful medicine before it's too late. You do not know what minute you may be overtaken by some dire calamity."

The medicine show era drew to a close in the 1930s. The newly formed U.S. Food and Drug Administration and

---

3. Though Hamlin's Wizard Oil was advertised as for external use only, for certain illnesses, customers were encouraged to ingest the medicine!

the Federal Trade Commission determined which drugs could be sold and which claims had to be eliminated because of false advertising. Automobiles and movie theaters meant people no longer had to wait for entertainment to find them; they could seek it out themselves. Easy access to drugstores meant regulated medicine was available to anyone who needed it.

While their claims might not be as bold or extravagant as they were in the past, cure-alls and charlatans still exist today. Listen carefully the next time you hear about an amazing pill or product. Listen and remember. No remedy can cure every ache or pain. No product can solve every problem. No person has all the answers.

A HISTORICAL NOTE

Language is a living thing that changes over time. When it comes to language used to describe race, there are some words that are never acceptable no matter the moment in history. Other terms that were once commonly used might seem surprising today. They can feel dated or even disrespectful, leaving us uncomfortable when we read or hear them. In 1887, when *Miraculous* takes place, many African Americans used "colored" to describe themselves. In the interest of accuracy, the term "colored" is used in this book.

Turn the page for an excerpt of

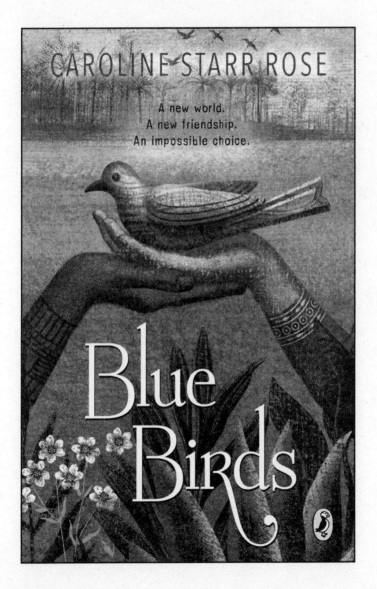

CAROLINE STARR ROSE

A new world.
A new friendship.
An impossible choice.

Blue
Birds

Alis

Almost three months we've journeyed,
each wave pushing us farther
from London,
every day moving us closer
to Virginia.

But now we're anchored on sandy banks
in a place we're not to be.

The enormity of our circumstance
comes crashing down around us.
Though this is Virginia,
it's not our new home.

We will be forced ashore
miles from where
our pilot, Ferdinando,
promised to take us.

Yet our Governor
does nothing to stop him.

Alis

How ready I am to leave this ship,
stretch my legs, be free!
But not like this,
tossed out
like yesterday's rubbish.

Father stands in the pinnace,
holds his hand to me.
"Come, Alis."
I step into the smaller boat,
less steady,
less sturdy.

Mother eases in,
cradling her belly,
perspiration at her temples,
her once-starched collar
dingy and askew.

"What will we do?" Mother whispers.
Her cheek rests on Father's shoulder.
"How will we reach the land
that's been promised us?"

"We'll find my brother and his men."

Uncle.
I grasp the wooden bird
in my pocket.
I did not dream
of seeing him so soon.
Surely he and the other soldiers
will set things right,
speak sense to Ferdinando.

Maybe he has already
caught sight of the boats,
will welcome us onshore.

Alis

Before me is a place
few Englishmen have ever seen.
I lean over the bow,
try to will the pinnace faster
to trees pointing heavenward,
a flock of cranes rippling the sky.
Mother grasps my plait,
gives my hair a tug.
"Careful," she says.

The boat cuts through the water
as wind snaps our sails,
rocks us with each wave
toward land heavy with trees,
thick with darkness.
The mysterious island,

Roanoke.

Alis

The pinnace drops anchor,
and that savage, Manteo,
offers me his hand,
the Indian who came to England
with the Governor
after his first voyage here.

I shake my head,
for even though he's lived in London
and dresses as we do,
I've seen the hair as long as a woman's
he hides underneath his hat.
I will not let him touch me.

My steps are uncertain
after our ocean crossing,
and when I stumble in the sand,
I ignore Manteo's amused smile,
choose not to stand but sit and watch
the scramble of people,
the rising tide,
the pinnace already making its way
back to the ships
for the last of us.

I scan the banks for Uncle Samuel,
but he is nowhere.

Alis

The Governor bids us to follow him
across the sandy beach.
Marsh grass swishes against my skirts.

     London's crowded streets
     smelled of rot and filth.
     I'd hold my breath,
     race my friend
     down Fish Street to London Bridge.
     Neither Joan nor I ever made it
     without pulling in deep gulps of air
     as putrid as death.

Here,
damp wood mingles
with the warm sea breeze.
The forest rises up,
takes us in,
and in the woods,
scattered all around,
pink flowers,
starred yellow in their centers,
tremble with each footstep.
I pluck a jaunty bloom,
tuck it behind my ear.

Even on summer days
the London light was weak,
fighting soot and drizzling clouds.

Here,
sunlit patches
cut through highest branches,
a brilliant red bird wings above.
Her sharp notes climb up,
spiral down.

In London stray dogs roam in mangy coats
scrounging for a scrap of meat.

Here,
waves lap the shore,
crabs dance across the sand,
berry bushes reach as high
as entryways at Bishop's Gate.

What a strange and wondrous place!

KIMI

They crash through the forest.
I crouch behind trees,
watching
as they
stumble
through underbrush.

Never did I think
these strange ones would return.
Yet here they are again.

Some think
they are spirits back from the dead.
Some say
they have invisible weapons
that strike with sickness after they've gone.

Father
said they were people
like us, only
with different ways.
But how can I believe him?

Father
is dead.

Alis

Ahead,
people gather in a clearing.
We must be near the settlement
where a few soldiers
lay claim for England.

Last year,
when Uncle left us,
he promised we wouldn't long be parted.
After his time in the Queen's service,
he'd be home again.
How surprised he'll be
to learn we've come!

I want to run ahead,
clutch him in a hug,
show him how faithfully
I've kept his wooden bird.

But my legs are unsteady.
Surely Mother needs me near.
The baby we await
fatigues her so easily.
Her face is worn.
Her golden hair
tumbles loose about her shoulders,
and I lace my arm through hers,
maybe hurry her more than she would wish,

but gently,
so as not to tire her more.

Governor White and his assistants draw together.
All about us
words clash and climb
until the Governor calls for silence.
Two men break away from the Governor's side.
He says they'll go ahead,
enter the settlement through the gate.

Even though I shouldn't,
I release Mother's arm,
drop my bundle at her feet.

"Alis!" she calls,
but I pretend I cannot hear her,
for I must find Uncle.

I skirt the crowd.
A fluttering blue bird draws me—
one with plumes as lavish as a gown.
I pray it leads me to him,
my uncle,
who knows so much of wild things,
but the bird escapes me.

Somehow
I've run
far beyond the others.

Somehow
I've reached a ditch
encircling an earthen barrier—
one ring inside another,
like the moat surrounding London Wall.
It isn't hard to slip down the ditch's side,
scale the embankment within,
and I'm in the settlement—
if this place could be called that—
with homes empty,
deer wandering through open doors,
vines twisting about windows.

Two of our men walk about,
one towering over the other,
whose nose is a mountain
of lumps and bumps.
I step back from view,
stumble,
fall into a heap of ash,
the charred remains of a building.

A scream
claws at my throat.

Bleached bones
litter the ground.

READY FOR ANOTHER HISTORICAL MYSTERY?

Keep reading for an excerpt of

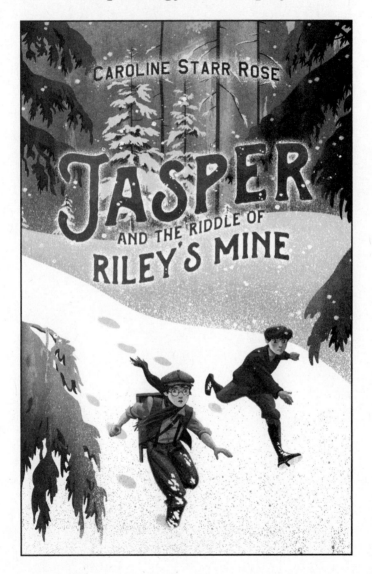

CHAPTER 1

The blanket over my head don't block out the sound, a tapping at the window sharp as hailstones. I roll over and try to get on back to sleep, but the noise gets louder. Then a second sound starts in, this one soft and breathy.

"Jasper," it says.

That ain't a storm I hear.

The room's dark, but a faint light glows outside, enough to see Pa's bed is as jumbled as usual. No telling, though, if he's in there or not.

"Come on, wake up," the voice whispers.

Melvin? My brother's on the porch? I listen close for that funny whistle Mel makes when he sleeps heavy, but don't hear it. Mel ain't in his bed like he should be.

A groan escapes Pa's lumpy blanket as three sharp raps

rattle the windowpane. Don't know how I missed him earlier, blowing in how he does, loud and clumsy as a blind moose. Usually mad as one, too. I grab my glasses, race across them worn floorboards as quick as I can, and crack open the door. There's my brother on the other side. He hoots and grins as he swings a newspaper over his head. The lantern he holds jitters, casting jagged shadows.

"You need to hush!" I slip out onto the porch, shut the door real gentle.

Mel quiets some, but he still dances around. If I didn't know him better, the way he's acting, pure crazy on his face, I'd think he'd got into Pa's liquor. Any second now I expect Pa to fly out of bed, cussing like a kicked cat, and knock some sense into him.

"Where've you been?" I take the lantern from Mel's hand, set it on the top step for safekeeping. "What're you doing out here, anyhow?"

"I was talking with the men at the wool mill and lost track of time." The lantern hardly gives off any light, but even so, Mel's eyes shine unnatural-like. He smiles as though he can't hardly help himself. "Then I had to get to Hansen's for a newspaper before the others beat me to it."

I don't know what Melvin's on about. "But it's the middle of the night."

"Jasper, there's something I've got to tell you that can't wait until morning. That's why I called you out here." Mel

2

glances at the darkened window. "I didn't want to wake Pa."

Mel ain't one to come home late, and he certainly don't run around all hours. My hands feel funny, all hot and cold at once. "What is it?"

"Wait till you see this." Mel smacks that newspaper he's holding. "Mr. Hansen sold me one of the very last copies."

We ain't had a newspaper for years. It's one of them luxuries we can't afford.

"'July 17, 1897,'" I read aloud. "'Latest News from the Klondike. Nine O'Clock Edition.'" It's this morning's *Seattle Post-Intelligencer*. The words run bold across the middle:

GOLD! GOLD! GOLD! GOLD!
SIXTY-EIGHT RICH MEN ON
THE STEAMER *PORTLAND*.
STACKS OF YELLOW METAL!

"Gold," I say again. The word feels warm and round and strange on my tongue.

Below the story is a map, a spiderweb of wavy lines that lead to a river labeled Klondike. The paper says the whole place is called the Klondike for the river that passes through. It's in some part of Canada far above

Washington, right up against Alaska, about as distant as the moon.

A light breeze ruffles Mel's sandy hair, sets the lantern flame to sputtering. "The paper says the *Portland* pulled into Seattle this morning," he says. "Everyone on board was loaded down with gold."

What I wouldn't give to see some gold up close. Only got to once before, a couple years ago, when Mama showed me Pa's pocket watch. "Think any of them fellows will come out to Kirkland and show us what they found?"

"No one will come to this nothing town." Mel loses his gooney look and puts on the practical face he wears near about all the time, the one where his eyebrows pinch together and his lips flatten into a firm line. "Don't know why I stay sometimes."

"Well, I do," I tell him. "You stick around because you've still got money to earn. You stay because of me."

Mel gives half his pay from the mill to Pa. What Pa don't know is that when he's out carousing, my brother pries back the loose floorboard under his bed and hides the other half in the cigar box Mama once used for recipes. He's saving for the two of us. As soon as he's got enough, we'll leave Kirkland together. Because here's the thing: ever since Mama left, Pa's gone from bad to worse.

Mel shoves his hands deep into his pockets. "I could save every penny I earn and come nowhere near what those men on the *Portland* have. A man in the Klondike makes more money in one week than I'll ever have in my whole life."

There's a prickly feeling at the back of my neck as I think on what Mel said. Gold's worth loads of money, and money's what we need. I don't know one family with enough, but even Cyril's, with them five kids, knows how to make a paycheck last. Once Pa touches the money Mel gives him, it's as good as gone. "There ain't no reason for us to wait," I say. "We could make it on our own right now. In the Klondike." I ain't ever been outside Kirkland, let alone Washington, and here's our chance to go. Not somewhere close by, neither, but to Canada, on the top of the world.

"Listen, Jasper." Mel steps away from me a bit. "About that."

"We could leave next week. Or even tomorrow." I can't slow down what's bubbling up inside. "Sure, I'd miss Cyril and fishing at the lake, and—"

"Jasper," Mel says. "You've got to listen to me."

That's when the front door swings open. Pa stands in the frame, tall and terrible. His eyes are bloodshot slits, his wild hair points in all directions. "Shut your traps," he says, "and put out that god-awful light! What're you boys doing, anyhow? Get inside and go to bed."

There ain't nothing we can do but obey.

My mind don't settle when I cross them floorboards that creak beneath me or when I climb in under my ragged quilt. Mel's whistle says he's drifted off long before that word quits echoing my heartbeat—gold, gold, gold.

Next morning, I'm extra quiet as I make my bed and boil the same coffee grounds I used yesterday. Second-day coffee ain't much different than hot water, but it's what I got to do to make the coffee stretch. There's no sense rattling Pa again, if I can help it. The newspaper Mel carried on about last night is spread across the table. I wrap my hands around my warm tin cup and dig right into the story about the gold. It says that a few days ago, a steamboat arrived in San Francisco, full of men called prospectors and their Klondike treasure. Word got out that another Klondike steamer named the *Portland* was headed to Seattle right behind them. News reporters were so hungry for the story, they rode a tugboat to meet the *Portland* offshore.

The coffee burns as I swallow it down. Men struck it rich last summer, and the rest of the world knew nothing about it until now—a whole *year* later.

The map below the story is called *The Land of Gold* and nearly covers the whole bottom half of the page. I run my finger over its wiggly river lines. There's so many of them. The biggest river, named the Yukon, starts in the mountains of Canada, then heads north and crosses into Alaska, which it cuts clear in half, then snakes west until it meets the sea. From the Yukon on the Canada side flows the Klondike River. The land south of it is where them men on the *Portland* made their fortunes, where me and Melvin are headed as soon as he says go.

Pa stumbles to the table and yanks the paper from me. I reach for my cup but can't steady it in time. Coffee spills everywhere. Pa holds the paper before him like he didn't just snatch it, like he's been reading it all morning. "Don't just sit there," he says. "Clean up that dripping mess."

That's Pa. He makes problems of his own and tells others to fix them. Ain't no way I'd answer back, though sometimes I sorely want to. Arguing with Pa leads to nothing but sorrow. That and the fire of his belt across my legs. Believe me, I don't run my mouth no more. I've learned that lesson good.

I wipe the table, then kneel down to clean the floor.

Pa fans the paper open. "Where'd you get this?"

"Mel brought it home from Hansen's yesterday."

"Mel." He shakes his head. "Throwing away money on a newspaper. And you. Don't know what you two were up to out there on the porch. Loud enough to wake the dead."

Pa's eyes are as dull as they were last night. He's got a stink like that mouse stuck in Miss Stapleton's desk all summer long. But even so, he don't seem too fierce this morning, not as riled as he could be. It's best to keep him that way.

I wring out the rags, set them aside for the laundry I'll have to get to soon.

"Bring me some coffee," Pa says. "And don't you leave a drop for that lazy brother of yours."

Mel stirs in his bed, like he's heard us talking. Ain't no way he couldn't in a house this small.

I hand Pa his cup as he hunches over the newspaper. He mutters to himself. "Klondike gold. Bunch of fools."

Mel shuffles to the stove in his red underdrawers, a union suit that bags around his kneecaps and has worn clean through at the elbows, and reaches for the empty coffeepot. He looks a sight. Probably didn't sleep a wink.

Pa lowers the paper. "You read this newspaper yet?"

Mel nods.

"You mark my words," Pa says. "Now that gold's been discovered in Canada, a whole load of idiots will head up there and try to find some for themselves."

I wonder what Pa will say when he learns me and Melvin plan to do exactly that.

Leave here. For good. To get us some gold.

"Them fellows are chumps," I chime in for Pa's sake. "Idiots." The whole time I say it, I make eyes at Mel, try to catch his notice and figure out what he's thinking. But all his attention's on Pa.

"It's the sort of man who ain't worked an honest day in his life that would try something so stupid," Pa says. "The type who wants things easy."

Mel holds the coffeepot like he's forgotten all about it. "What's so easy about leaving everything you know?"

I want to swat my brother with a dishrag, step on his toes and make him holler, anything to draw him back, because this conversation ain't headed nowhere good. Melvin should be quiet after last night's hooting and dancing on the porch.

But he plows ahead. "Familiar is what's easy. It's brave to leave what you know behind."

Pa's lip curls. "You contradicting me, boy?"

I grab the broom, busy myself with the dust that's crept in under the door, get as far as I can from whatever storm Mel's stirring up with Pa. Of course I want to tell Pa exactly what I think, ask him straight out what he remembers about honest work when it's surprising if he gets himself to his job at Hansen's more than a few days a week. But I ain't stupid, either.

Lay low and stay out of the way, that's the rule around here. Melvin taught it to me when Pa lost his job at the mill six months before he got his own there. Mel's always been the one to keep the peace, the one who slows Pa's anger when my mouth runs on its own. So how come all of a sudden Mel's acting like he's forgotten everything?

Mel slams the empty pot on the stove.

"I said"—Pa's words are sharp and loud—"are you contradicting me?"

Mel still don't answer. He stomps straight from the kitchen, pulls out his crate of clothes from underneath his bed, yanks on his trousers, and shoves his arms through his shirtsleeves. The whole time he mumbles but don't look once at Pa.

Oh, my heart thunders to see him act so reckless.

"Don't you talk under your breath," Pa says. "You got something to tell me, Melvin Johnson, you say it outright."

That gets him to stop. Something about Mel looks almost grown, him who's barely sixteen. "Who are you to judge the man who wants a better life?"

"Who am I?" Pa lunges forward. His hand flies out, strikes Melvin square on the cheek. "I'm your pa. Don't you ever forget it."

I duck behind the table, my fists balled up so tight, my fingernails cut through my skin. "Hush, Mel, hush. Just hush," I say.

Mel's face burns red where Pa hit him, but he don't stop. "You want to know what they say about you at the mill, Pa? That you're good-for-nothing. That once Mama died, you took to drinking like it was the only thing you remembered how to do."

"Don't you bring your mama into this!" Pa bellows. He moves in so close, Mel's backed against the wall.

"You could have saved her." Mel's eyes flash. "You could have if you'd wanted to."

I hold my hands against my ears, but it don't keep their voices out.

Pa's like a firecracker set to explode. "What do you mean, if I'd wanted to?"

"You could have taken help the first time it was offered. But you didn't." Mel's jaw is clenched, and his head's pressed hard on the wooden boards behind him. "Want to know what else the men at the mill told me?" He takes a breath and lets it out slow. "They say I'm the one who's the real man around here."

Pa storms across the room, grabs for the empty coffee-pot, and lets it fly. It hits inches from Mel's head. Brown streaks run down the wall. The pot clatters to the floor.

Mel's face is a mix of fear and anger, but anger wins out quick. He jerks the door open and slams it from the other side.

Pa lowers himself into Mama's rocker, still angled near the window the way she always liked it.

I stand on shaky legs. There's too much sadness in this house. More ugliness than I can bear. How I itch to be anywhere else.

Pa looks past the window, unblinking. There ain't no trace of the caring fellow he used to be.

The wool mill hisses and clatters the morning me and Cyril walk past, loud as Mel's been quiet since last month's fight with Pa.

Cyril peers again at the fish in my bucket. "You'll eat fine tonight." Three perch and a smallmouth bass, their sides splotched gray and yellow, flop against the bucket's sides. Cyril grins. His chapped lips don't fit too good around his crooked teeth. "Sure beats my scrawny trout."

"Mel better be home before suppertime if he wants to eat tonight. Pa don't let me keep food out for him no more."

Since that awful morning him and Pa fought, Mel's kept to himself. He leaves early for the mill and gets home long after I'm in bed. Every night I take Mel's newspaper from under my pillow and read through the gold story one more time. I'm set to ask Mel about our Klondike plans—what we'll bring and when we'll leave and how we'll work around Pa—just as soon as I catch him alone.

"Meet you at the lake tomorrow morning?" Cyril asks.

I nod. "See you then."

Cyril swings his bucket as he goes.

The August sun ain't reached its full height, but already it blazes like it means business. My footsteps ring hollow on the porch steps. The house is dark and still. Could be Pa's already left to work at Hansen's.

"Wondered where you were," Pa says as I open the door. He tucks in his ragged shirt and pulls up his suspenders, like he's just made a start to his morning when the day is pushing toward noon.

"I caught four fish for supper." The water slops in the bucket as I lift it to the cupboard.

That's when I see the letter propped against the empty

flour jar. The letter's in Mel's hand. There ain't no reason for him to write a note unless something's wrong.

Pa leans in to study his supper. Quick as that, I push past to grab the letter.

"What was that for?" Pa growls. "You could have knocked over them fish."

"Just checking to see if there's enough flour for biscuits." I reach for the empty jar and give it a shake. "Nope." When Pa ain't looking, I work Mel's note into my pocket.

Pa starts in on how tired he is of perch, how any decent man deserves a bit of variety from time to time when it comes to his supper, but I don't really listen. I'm thinking about that letter.

Pa grips my shoulder, squeezes awful hard. "You hear what I said? I want them fish fried up when I get home. No saving some for Melvin, either. If he wants to eat, he better get back at a regular hour."

"Yes, sir," I say.

The place where Pa's hand pressed aches long after he lets up.

Pa eases himself into a chair to lace his boots. That letter feels like it's burning a hole clean through my trousers. Maybe I could hold it low behind the kitchen counter so Pa don't notice.

I slip it from my pocket, try to smooth it across my leg to work the wrinkles out. *Dear Pa,* it begins, *it's time for me to go.*

I don't read no more. I can't because my head don't make sense of them words. It's like each one's been flipped over and turned around.

Time to go. The letter says.

For me. Not "me and Jasper."

My name ain't mentioned at all.

"Boy, have you listened to a word I said?" Pa's on his feet again. He motions to my hand. "What's that you got?"

"It ain't nothing." I cram Mel's letter deep in my pocket. "What did you say?"

"I said you'd better see to them fish." Pa chews the inside of his cheek, eyeing me. "Mind yourself, Jasper. I'm low on patience." Pa tugs on his cap, and then he's out the door.

I wait and wait to be sure Pa's truly gone before I try Mel's letter again.

Dear Pa,

It's time for me to go.

Since I brought home that newspaper, all I've thought about is the gold that's been found in Canada. This is my chance, and I'm going to take it.

I know a sixteen-year-old boy's old enough to be on his own. You've said as much a hundred times. But I've stuck around to help out. Mainly I've kept on

because of Jasper. He's acted strong since he got
over the influenza, but he's eleven, Pa. A kid. Be
good to him. That's all I ask. If not for me, then for
Mama.

Your son,
Melvin Johnson

An awful feeling squeezes my middle. Melvin's gone. After that talk we had last month, after two years of promises we'd make our way together, he's up and left without me.

What was he thinking to leave me like that?

This is his chance, Mel says. His alone. It don't take long before my blood runs hot. I crumple up that letter, swing my arm hard as I can. The paper ball bounces off the door, rolls under Melvin's bed.

So I'm just some little kid. Oh, that Melvin thinks he's something special, how he holds a job and knows what's happening in the world outside of Kirkland. Miss Stapleton still loves to talk about what a perfect student he was, but that don't mean he knows everything.

I got more sense than ten Mels put together plus a couple more. He thinks he's practically a man, can do what he pleases. But what kind of a man makes promises, then runs off the first chance he gets?

As I reach for Mel's note, the loose floorboard beneath

his bed jiggles. I pry it back, and there's the cigar box, where it's always been. Except it's cleaned out. Empty. The crate of clothes Mel stores under there, that's empty, too. His two books are missing. The knapsack he keeps on a hook is gone.

But there's one real important thing he's left behind.

His extra pair of underdrawers sits right on top of yesterday's clean laundry, the red union suit with the worn-through elbows and the baggy knees. Serves him right to be stuck with only one set of underwear. Old Mel ain't as clever as he thinks he is.

Up there in the Klondike in his one pair of underclothes, how's he gonna get along? With the newspaper map under my pillow, he won't be able to find his way.

And then I remember. Pa's pocket watch.

Mama showed it to me and Mel one winter afternoon while rain streamed down the windows and thunder shivered the walls. It was a few months after Pa lost his job. Mama told us to sell the watch if ever me and Mel found ourselves in a tough spot. We didn't ask how come she could decide about something that belonged to Pa. She knew how hard things were for us. I'm glad she ain't seen how bad it's gotten.

I lift the corner of the quilt on Pa's bed, dig around beneath his straw-tick mattress until my hand closes on a lump of flannel. The gold watch is wrapped inside, all smooth and shiny.

So Mel didn't take it. That was always the plan. When the two of us lit out, we'd take that watch with us in case we ever got in any trouble. We meant to sell it if we were in a pinch and needed money quick.

Mel's heading to Canada on his own. Sure, he's got some money, but he don't got this. I'm the one who can bring it to him. The truth is Melvin needs me. And more than anything, I'm owed an explanation on why he up and left without me.

It don't take long for me to pack. All I've got is a change of clothes, a coat, my green muffler, three pairs of Pa's woolen socks, the fifty-seven cents I won from Cyril on a dare, my school pencil, the front page of the *Seattle Post-Intelligencer*, and the last hunk of bread from me and Mel's secret stash. That red pair of underdrawers Mel's forgotten sits folded up real nice on top of yesterday's laundry. I can't wait to see his face, all grateful and embarrassed, when I hand them over.

But it's not the underdrawers my hand goes for first. It's Mama's washboard. Every time I hold it, I can't help but run my fingers over its middle, which zings with a sound almost like music. This washboard's one of the only things we still own that once belonged to her, and I ain't got the heart to leave it behind. Pa ain't partial to cleanliness. He won't notice it's missing, anyhow.

I drop Pa's watch in my pocket, grab those underdrawers, and strap the washboard to my pack. Mel's got a good head start on me. If I'm gonna catch up to him, I best be going myself. I'm halfway across the porch before I turn around. Pa may be a mess and is as mean as they come, but I took his watch. Sure, I got Mama's blessing, but that don't mean he knows it. The least I can do is tell him what's going on.

The front page of the newspaper's in my pocket folded around my pencil, but I've left the rest on the table. I write a note down one side.

Pa,

That gold up in Canada. Me and Mel are gone to get some.

Jasper

PS — I got the watch.

Then I hightail it out of there.

ACKNOWLEDGMENTS

As always, my deepest gratitude goes to Tracey Adams, my literary champion and advocate, and Stacey Barney, who challenges me to do my best work and helps me believe I'll (eventually!) succeed. Thank you to the team at Penguin Young Readers Group for your tireless efforts to create beautiful, meaningful books for children.

I invited my critique group members Stephanie Farrow, Katherine Hauth, Mark Karlins, Uma Krishnaswami, and Vaunda Micheaux Nelson into this story when it was little more than a few shaky chapters. Again and again their writerly wisdom helped me find my way. Thank you, friends, for the hand you played in shaping *Miraculous*. I couldn't have written this book without you.

Sadly, six months before *Miraculous* published, Mark Karlins passed away. He encouraged me to always look for the deeper story, once telling me "part of writing poetry and prose is allowing the writing to make mistakes, to fail (and then, with a little luck and humility, recover)." Thank you, Mark, for all you taught me. It was a gift to call you my friend.

Early on in my drafting, when I wasn't sure I was capable of the work I knew this novel would require, my critique partner, Valerie Geary, told me, "You have all the tools and all the knowledge and all the courage you need to write this book. You are not a scared writer. You are brave every time you come to the page." Val, I've returned to your words many times over the years. They're pinned on the wall over my desk. Thank you for letting me borrow your belief in me.

A thank-you also goes out to Terry Lynn Johnson, who read *Miraculous* (and many of my other books) in an earlier form. And thank you, Craig Phillips, for another wonderful cover. If I were to find my book on a shelf, I'd want to read it!

I'm indebted to a lecture about quacks, charlatans, and con men I stumbled upon while visiting a St. Louis museum the summer of 2013; David McRaney's books, *You Are Not So Smart* and *You Are Now Less Dumb*, about why we believe what we do and how these ideas lead us to act in certain ways; Anna-Lisa Cox's *The Bone and Sinew of the Land: America's Forgotten Black Pioneers and the Struggle for Equality*, which taught me about the rich history of Blacks in the Midwest; Anne Anderson's fascinating *Snake Oil, Hustlers, and Hambones: The American Medicine Show*, and the incomparable L. M. Montgomery, who always peppered her books with a wealth of memorable characters.

Like Mr. Ogden, my husband lives with early-onset Parkinson's disease (a movement disorder once called the shaking palsy that is characterized by tremors, stiffness in the limbs, and problems with balance). Thank you, Dan, for the dignity and determination and ridiculous humor you bring to our days. I'm so glad we're a team.

A final thanks to my young readers. It is my greatest privilege to write for you.

As I've worked on *Miraculous*, a quote by author and theologian Frederick Buechner has often come to mind. It encompasses what I hope this book (and, ideally, all my writing) conveys: "Here is the world. Beautiful and terrible things will happen. Don't be afraid."